Where were *you* when the clock struck twelve?

Colin Spencer, heir to the Spencer fortune, has finally chosen a bride. But he hadn't counted on the millennium bug—and free-spirited Isabelle Channing—to wreak havoc on his well-ordered life....

Isabelle Channing is congratulating herself on saving Maggie from marrying the wrong man. But now that she's married stuffy, sexy Colin herself, he doesn't seem to be so wrong....

Maggie Kelley, Colin's fiancée, wants some answers. Can she ever forgive Colin for accidentally marrying her best friend?

Luke Fitzpatrick has just realized how much he loves Maggie. And he's determined to get her to the altar before Colin changes his mind....

Four lives. Four loves.
One date with destiny.

Dear Reader,

Welcome to the year 2000! It's a brand-new century and Harlequin Temptation is ready to celebrate. We've got two fabulous linked stories by fan favorite Kate Hoffmann, both set on the most romantic night of the year.

New Year's Eve. December 31, 1999. It's the eve of the new millennium. Legend says the person you're with at the stroke of midnight is "the one." So what happens when sassy Isabelle Channing finds herself stuck in an elevator with stuffy Colin, her best friend's fiancé, *and* a bottle of bubbly? Find out in #762, *Always a Hero*, the sexy sequel to #758, *Once a Hero* (Dec. '99).

I hope you enjoy both of these great books. As a treat for our overseas readers, the books will be published around the world at the same time as in North America. Truly, love can be a universal experience!

Lastly, I hope you have exciting plans to celebrate the millennium. Whether it's an elegant party, a trip to Hawaii or just curling up by the fire with a Temptation novel, I hope the new century brings you love, peace and happiness.

Warmly,

Birgit Davis-Todd
Senior Editor
Harlequin Temptation

Kate Hoffmann
ALWAYS A HERO

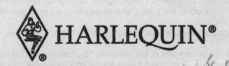

HARLEQUIN®

TORONTO • NEW YORK • LONDON
AMSTERDAM • PARIS • SYDNEY • HAMBURG
STOCKHOLM • ATHENS • TOKYO • MILAN • MADRID
PRAGUE • WARSAW • BUDAPEST • AUCKLAND

ISBN 0-373-25862-3

ALWAYS A HERO

Dear Reader,

When an event comes around only once in a thousand years, the temptation to put it in a book is irresistible. But little did I know when I started *Once a Hero* and *Always a Hero,* these books would become a small part of a worldwide celebration.

As you read *Always a Hero,* there are a thousand others just like you, scattered all over the world, reading this book at the same time. Romance has become a universal language thanks to dedicated readers—and to all the people at Harlequin who help bring my books to you.

When I think of how far my stories have traveled, and how many people they've entertained, I can't help but think of the editors, translators and sales staffs in countries that seem so far away from my tiny little office in Wisconsin. Yet, they're the ones who send me to places as distant as Poland and the Philippines, and Spain and Singapore.

So, let me raise a glass of fictional champagne to all the people who put this book in your hands—thanks for bringing us all together!

Happy New Year,

Kate Hoffmann

For everyone in the Harlequin offices throughout the world, who help my books travel from my heart to my readers' imaginations.

And with special thanks to Sue Schoenfeld, my expert on Las Vegas, and Andy Schleifer, my expert on divorce law.

1

COLIN SPENCER didn't know what all the fuss was about. After all, the new millennium was no more than a flip of a calendar page. Today it was 1999 and tomorrow would be 2000. Maybe the new year would be a problem for computers, but not for him. Tomorrow would be just another day—except he'd be officially engaged to be married.

All around him workers rushed to put the finishing touches on the grandest New Year's Eve party the city of Chicago had ever seen—though the vast majority of Chicago's population hadn't received an invitation. His mother, Eunice Spencer, had been working on plans for her grand millennium ball since last New Year's Day, determined to spend her way onto the society pages yet another time.

She'd done everything in her power to turn the top floor of the Spencer Center into her idea of a futuristic society event, going so far as to plan an elaborate laser-light show for the big moment. In truth, Colin hoped all the dire predictions of power outages and communications breakdowns might be unfounded. He was rather looking forward to seeing Eunice's extravaganza.

But there would be something even more exciting for the society gossips to talk about besides a laser-light show. Just before midnight, one of Chicago's most eligible bachelors would be pulled from the marriage market. Colin Spencer, heir to the vast Spencer fortune, had chosen a bride.

He stared across the ballroom at a slender figure in an ice-blue ball gown. Maggie Kelley patiently spoke to one of the caterers as several workers maneuvered a giant ice sculpture of the numeral 2000 atop an equally giant ice rendering of the Chicago skyline. There seemed to be some concern about the Sear's Tower, but Maggie was quite capable of ironing out the problem on her own.

Colin smiled to himself. She really was the perfect choice for a bride. She was sweet and even-tempered, and she managed to tolerate his parents well enough. And they shared a deep respect and affection for each other, though Colin couldn't exactly call it a grand passion.

He'd never really trusted in love. In Colin's opinion, choosing a wife should be based on more than just physical desire and emotional dependence. As far as he was concerned, a marriage was like a business partnership. Choices must be made based on common sense and acquired wisdom, after careful consideration of all the facts and the available options. Maggie Kelley just happened to be the best option when it came to a lifelong companion.

And the best thing was, she shared his pragmatic views on marriage. Together, they'd build a stable relationship that would include an expensive house in an exclusive neighborhood, two or three children and an undisputed spot as one of Chicago's most prominent couples.

"She may not come from money, but she's pretty enough. How are her teeth?"

Colin shifted his gaze off his fiancé and turned to his father. Edward Spencer scowled as he studied Maggie Kelley shrewdly, his bushy white eyebrows meeting in the middle of his forehead. Colin couldn't remember the last time he'd seen his father smile. Considering the amount Eunice Spencer had dropped on this party, Colin didn't expect that it would be anytime soon.

"She's not a polo pony," he muttered.

"If she were, at least we'd know what she was made of," Edward replied. "She'd come with papers, bloodlines. You say both her parents are dead?"

Colin's eyes drifted from Maggie to the elegantly appointed ballroom. Four hundred of Chicago's wealthiest and most influential would arrive in less than an hour to help ring in the new millennium—every guest with more impeccable breeding than the hosts of the party. In truth, Edward Spencer was considered new money, but new money was deemed acceptable to the elite of Chicago as long as it came in quantities greater than their own.

Colin detested all the social posturing and the petty maneuvering that went on at these events, though they were a necessary evil that came along with family wealth. He could just imagine the buzz that would go up after his parents announced the engagement of their only son right before the stroke of midnight.

No one would know who Maggie Kelley was or where she came from. They'd question her connections and her motives and there might even be talk of an unplanned pregnancy. Colin knew it would be rough for a while as the gossips got used to the notion he was marrying beneath his class. But he wasn't about to choose one of those mercenary beauties his mother had trotted in front of him, single daughters from prominent families looking to snare themselves a wealthy and powerful husband.

With Maggie, he knew exactly what he was getting. A woman who was satisfied just to have a pleasant home and a chance to start a family. She wouldn't ask for more than happiness and security, a safe future with a husband who cared for her. The money meant nothing to Maggie and that's exactly why he had decided to marry her—that and the fact there wouldn't be any in-laws that came along in the bargain.

"She never knew her father," Colin said. "Her mother died five years ago."

"You could have selected someone from our own social circle," Edward said.

Colin chuckled. "Like you did? You seem to forget my mother's father was the son of a butcher. She didn't have money and you married her anyway."

"That's because I didn't have money," Edward said. "But you do. *My* money. And money changes everything."

Colin shook his head. There were no truer words. If it hadn't been for the money, Colin could have lived a completely different life. He could have been a fireman or a policeman, like he'd dreamed of being when he was seven. But his life had been determined from the moment of his birth. He was brought into the world to take over Spencer Enterprises, to increase the family wealth and continue the family line. And he couldn't do that until he was happily married with a wife and children of his own.

"I hope you told her about the prenuptial," Edward said.

"There won't be a prenup," Colin replied. "I didn't mention it and I don't plan to. If Maggie thinks I'd even consider divorce, she'd never agree to marry me in the first place. As far as we're both concerned, this marriage is for a lifetime."

Though the words sounded appropriate, Colin couldn't help but wonder what he was getting himself into. A lifetime was forever. Was he really ready to admit his life was essentially over? He'd made all his life choices by the time he was thirty-four. What was left but to show up at the same office, day after day, and spend his hours making the family more money? When he looked at it objectively, the whole prospect was rather dismal.

Colin drew in a sharp breath. There was no going back. If he wanted to run Spencer Enterprises, he'd have to provide his father with the necessary prerequisites—most importantly, the next generation of Spencers. "If you want me to marry, you have to let me do it my way. Maggie's willing to join this family. The least I can do is risk a little of the family money in return."

His father grumbled for a few seconds, then sniffed. "Then you better be sure you made the right choice."

"I have," Colin replied. "I promise."

He sighed inwardly. Colin could hardly believe the eve of the millennium was upon them. While everyone else in the world was making their own resolutions, Colin couldn't help but see the irony in his own choices. When he thought back on his life, he never would have predicted he'd end up here, following so closely in his father's footsteps. What had happened to the promises he'd made himself? The promises to build his own life, to make his own choices, independent of family expectations.

When he'd graduated from college, he'd had every intention of walking away from a future that had been so carefully mapped out for him. But he'd taken a job with his father right after graduation, hoping to make a little more money before he made his break.

"It's now or never," Colin murmured, an unbidden dagger of doubt piercing his composure. He was about to announce his engagement! After that, there would be no going back. Just once before he cashed it all in, he'd like to let loose, to forget he was Colin Spencer. He knew what his friends thought of him—straitlaced, uptight, in control. "Predictable," he added.

"What are you mumbling about?"

His father's voice startled him out of his thoughts. "Nothing."

Edward tugged on the lapels of his tuxedo, his forehead knitted in concern. "I don't like this," he finally said. "We're tempting fate with this millennium bug, this Y2K business. What if the power goes out? What are we going to do with four hundred people stuck in a dark ballroom with no way to get out?"

"I briefed security and everything should be fine. The generator will kick in a few seconds after power loss. Nothing will spoil Mother's big event."

"Except that psychic fortune-teller palm-reader woman she hired for this party. Entertainment," he scoffed. "With a name like Madame Babushka, she's probably a con artist looking for an easy mark."

"I think it's Madame Blavatka."

"Go check her out," Edward ordered. "Make sure she's not out to fleece the guests. We don't want her doing something to embarrass your mother."

"And how am I supposed to figure that out?" Colin asked. "It's a little late for security to run a background check."

"Tell her to read your fortune," Edward ordered. "If she asks for money or says anything off-color, show her the door."

Colin nodded, then wandered across the room toward the psychic's table. He wasn't sure he wanted to hear what the future held for him, not that he believed in psychics. Her predictions would probably just confirm his own forecast for the rest of his life. He glanced over to see Maggie standing in the doorway, watching him. She sent him a smile and a quick wave.

He returned her smile, silently chastising himself. He was lucky to find a woman like Maggie. Over time, the affection and respect they shared might lead to more passionate feelings. And they could add a little excitement to their lives if they wanted, couldn't they? He made a mental note to plan a vacation as soon as his work schedule allowed.

"You've come to hear your future."

He glanced up to find himself standing at the fortune-teller's table. She pointed to an embroidered chair in front of the table, her bracelets jangling an exotic counterpoint to the big band tuning up at the other end of the reception hall.

"Please, sit. You are curious," she said. Her voice was heavy with an accent Colin was unable to place, although it sounded more southside Chicago than authentic Eastern European Gypsy. "Give me your palm. We will start there."

Colin reluctantly gave Madame Blavatka his hand, then waited impatiently while she went through her drill. First she examined his palm closely, then she feigned surprise, a look of amazement suffusing her heavily made-up face. "You have the mark," she said.

"Don't you mean, I *am* the mark?" he asked in a cynical tone.

She narrowed her eyes, anger flashing there for a moment. Then she dropped his hand. "I don't read the future for those who don't believe."

Colin laughed. "All right, all right. I believe. For now. Tell me my future."

"As I said, you have the mark. The mark of the millennium." She pointed to a spot near the base of his thumb. "These lines form a star. It's very unusual. This is the first time I've seen it."

"And what does it mean? Am I doomed to an early death? Or will I inherit millions?"

"At midnight tonight, you will look into the eyes of destiny," she said. "The instant the next millennium begins, you will be with the woman you are meant to spend your life with."

"Maggie?"

"I don't know her name. But you will share a passion, a burning love, that will never die."

He pulled his hand away, leaned back in his chair and crossed his arms over his chest. "So who told you I was engaged? Was my mother filling your ear with pertinent gossip about all the guests?"

"You think I'm a charlatan? You will see," Madame Blavatka said, wagging her finger. "All will be revealed at midnight. Now, go. I have no time for skeptics."

"How much do I owe you for the advice?"

She brushed him off with a wave of her hand. "I want no money. Just the satisfaction of knowing I'm right."

Colin pushed back the chair and stood. "Since I'm announcing my engagement just before midnight, your chances for a hit on this one are pretty high."

"Not everything goes as planned," she said, reaching for her crystal ball. "Destiny has a way of surprising us."

Colin took his billfold from his pocket and tossed a few dollars on the table. "Thanks. I'll keep that in mind."

As he stepped away from the table, he noticed the first guests had begun to arrive. Colin glanced at his watch then shook his head. He'd hoped to spend a little time with Maggie before the party got under way. With all his business associates invited, he'd need to devote most of the evening to mingling with them.

Luckily, Maggie had invited guests of her own. Though Isabelle Channing had an irritating habit of insulting him whenever she could, she was one of Maggie's closest friends. Isabelle was audacious and outspoken and she had entirely too much influence on Maggie. But when the two of them got together, nothing could separate them.

And there was Luke Fitzpatrick, who would no doubt stay by Maggie's side, ever the hero to Maggie's damsel in distress. Colin should have felt a little jealous, but he didn't. Maggie and Luke had been friends since they were kids and she relied on him as if he were her big brother. Besides, it had been Luke who'd introduced Maggie to Colin two years ago, so there was really no cause for any petty feelings of resentment or envy. In truth, Colin was glad Maggie would have an escort for the party so he could concentrate on other matters.

Colin rubbed the back of his neck with his hand, working at the knot of tension growing there. Suddenly, he felt as if he was suffocating. Turning toward the terrace door, Colin took a deep breath then let it out slowly. Now was no time for second thoughts. He'd chosen his course for the rest of his life and there was no turning back.

When the clock struck midnight, the new millennium would begin. Nothing, not even a bout of cold feet, could stop time from marching on.

ISABELLE CHANNING SLIPPED out of her wrap and tossed it on the coat-check counter outside the reception area, then grabbed her ticket and tucked it in her purse. Thankfully, most of the guests had already arrived at Eunice Spencer's Millennium Eve Ball. She hated walking into a party with only half the guests present—no one would notice her entrance and she'd spent far too much time on her gown to let it go unappreciated.

She glanced down and smoothed the formfitting skirt. She had taken her cue from a costume she'd designed for the Shakespeare Theatre Company's production of *Antony and Cleopatra*. Egyptian in style, the crimson gown was covered with elaborate beading and brilliant hand-coloring. A headdress probably would have been appropriate, but Isabelle didn't want to draw too much attention to herself, so she'd

pulled her dark hair back into a neat chignon.
Makeup and elaborate earrings finished off the look.

As she stepped into the ballroom, her breath
caught in her throat. High above Michigan Avenue,
Chicago's rich and famous had turned out for what
the society columns would no doubt call the party of
the year. Everything glittered, from the table cover-
ings to the designer gowns to the yards of silver net-
ting that surrounded the floor-to-ceiling columns.
Flowers decorated nearly every available surface,
and uniformed waiters bearing silver trays wove
through the crowd. She glanced up and found the
ceiling covered with thousands of tiny white lights,
creating a canopy of stars.

Isabelle could see she was the only one of Chicago's impoverished and obscure to be invited. She'd
known Maggie Kelley for four years, since they'd
met in a watercolor class at the Art Institute, during
the height of Isabelle's self-improvement phase. If it
weren't for Maggie, Isabelle would probably be
spending the turn of the millennium with a box of
chocolates and a romantic video, bemoaning the fact
she'd have no one to kiss. But here she was, tossed
into a crowd of society men, each one of them emi-
nently kissable.

"Oh, Mother, wouldn't you be so proud of your
little Isabelle now." She could almost imagine the
squeal of delight issuing from her mother's mouth
had she known Isabelle was invited to such an important party. She glanced over the crowd, searching
for the customary photographers who attended these
events. If she tried hard enough, she might be able to
horn her way into a photo opportunity. Her smiling
face staring out from the pages of *Town and Country*

would probably drive Camille Channing into fits of ecstasy.

But then, she hadn't come here to make her mother happy. Marrying a rich doctor was the only way she could accomplish that. She'd come to Eunice Spencer's Millennium Ball to have fun! She planned to kiss as many handsome men as possible along the way. And if those plans went awry, at least she'd have Luke Fitzpatrick to kiss—if he decided to show up.

Luke was her unofficial date for the evening and she used the term quite loosely. He'd agreed to accompany her to the party but he'd called at the last moment to beg off with problems at work. Isabelle had been forced to cab it over to Michigan Avenue with only a weak promise from him that he'd try to make it before midnight.

Knowing Luke, he'd do his best. After all, it was Maggie Kelley's invitation that held more weight with him than a date with Isabelle Channing. Maggie and Luke were as tight as any siblings could be, though they shared not a drop of common blood. Isabelle chalked up their bond to the shared experiences of childhood.

Isabelle sighed. If Luke didn't show up, she'd have to find another candidate for the big kiss before the first notes of "Auld Lang Syne" rolled through the ballroom. There was nothing more pitiful than an odd girl out at a New Year's Eve party, standing on the sidelines while everyone locked lips. And she wasn't about to start the new millennium off on the wrong foot!

She strolled along the buffet table and plucked a few tidbits from the vast spread of elegant hors d'oeuvres. As she munched on a stuffed pea pod, Isabelle noticed Colin Spencer standing in the midst of a group of tuxedoed gentlemen.

Isabelle found a spot near a huge pillar and studied Colin covertly. She'd always wondered about him. She had never met anyone as tightly strung as Spencer. He was always so cool and composed, his suits impeccably tailored, his shirts pressed and his underwear stiffly starched. Every time she saw him, she had to fight the urge to mess up his hair and twist his tie and kick dust on his perfectly shined shoes. Colin Spencer seemed like a man who could use a little chaos in his life. Maybe then he'd start to act human.

They shared an uneasy alliance, their only common ground being Maggie Kelley. Isabelle knew Colin didn't approve of her bohemian lifestyle or her wild ways. He found her behavior unsuitable and he took every opportunity to discourage Maggie from associating with her.

As for Isabelle, she had to feel a little sorry for Colin Spencer. Though the package was pretty, the contents were as unappealing as day-old porridge. Sure, he dressed beautifully and he had a body to die for. And those perfectly flawless features—the straight nose and chiseled mouth. What girl wouldn't be impressed?

Not Isabelle Channing! Colin was exactly the type of man her mother had always touted. Safe, dependable and worth a few million. He acted as if the world belonged to him by mere virtue of his wealth. And he treated Maggie like just another one of his possessions. Thank goodness Maggie had remained somewhat immune to his charms. Here was a man whose every ounce of passion was so consumed by making more money that he didn't have anything left for romance.

The corners of Isabelle's mouth curled up in a smile as she continued to watch Colin. What would he do if she planted a big, wet kiss on *his* lips at midnight? Maybe even stuck her tongue in his mouth. Could she get him to blush? Would he actually give in to embarrassment or would he maintain his cool? She pressed her finger to her chin as she pondered the possibility. The kiss would probably be quite uninspiring on his part—dry, a little tense, maybe impassive. Very proper and chaste.

Still, it would be fun to try. There was a certain excitement in tempting such a straitlaced guy. All the other men she'd dated were so easy. A coy look, a flirtatious smile, a fleeting caress and they'd be lost. But it would take more to bewitch a guy like Colin.

A pea pod caught in her throat and she swallowed hard, then coughed. Not that she'd ever try anything like that with her best friend's boyfriend! Isabelle had done some outrageous things in her life, but she'd never do anything to hurt Maggie. Maggie was the most loyal friend she'd ever had.

Isabelle dragged her gaze away from Colin and caught sight of Maggie across the ballroom. She stood alone at the edge of the dance floor, looking a little forlorn. Leave it to Colin to abandon her without a second thought. Isabelle grabbed a few more nibbles from the buffet table and headed across the dance floor. On the way, she snatched a noisemaker from a table full of party favors and a glass of champagne from a passing waiter.

Without a word, she sidled up to Maggie and followed her friend's gaze to the spot where Colin stood. With a playful giggle, she blew the party horn near Maggie's ear, drawing her attention away from the handsome stiff in the tux.

Startled, Maggie pressed her palm to her chest and turned. "Isabelle!"

"Don't look so glum," Isabelle mocked with a droll lift of her eyebrow. "At midnight, little green aliens will descend on this party and turn all these bluebloods into pod people. It's a millennium prophecy, haven't you heard?" Isabelle pushed the plate of hors d'oeuvres into Maggie's hand. "This food is to die for. Old Eunice sure knows how to put out a spread."

Maggie popped a shrimp into her mouth and studied the crowd thoughtfully. "Have you noticed? None of these women eat. That's one more thing I'll have to master. Sophisticated starvation."

"Maybe they're already pod people. Pod people don't eat. And they do look a little...vacuous."

Maggie giggled. "Compared to you, *everyone* looks a little lifeless."

Isabelle smiled. "Thank you. I'm glad at least one person appreciates my gown." Isabelle pressed her wrist to her forehead and struck a pose. "I designed it myself."

Isabelle had always loved clothes—not buying them, but designing them and constructing them. She'd run through nearly every job in the fashion industry before settling in at the costume shop for the Shakespeare Theatre Company. She'd begun as a lowly dresser, then moved up to seamstress. Five years ago, they'd allowed her to design the extras' costumes for a new production of *A Midsummer*

Night's Dream. The project had given her the chance to prove her talent and, within a year, she'd been named head designer.

Her tastes had always run to the theatrical when it came to her own wardrobe choices. She glanced at Maggie's elegant ice-blue gown. It was a perfect choice for her pale complexion and ash-blond hair. But Isabelle needed color, bold, brilliant color. Sparkle and dazzle that caused heads to turn and people to talk.

"You obviously haven't resolved to start dressing conservatively for the new millennium," Maggie murmured with a teasing smile.

"Oh, no," Isabelle replied. "But I did make a few other resolutions. I've resolved to give up topless bathing on North Beach. And I won't be mouthing off to policemen in the next year. I've also decided to stop dating policemen who arrest me for indecent exposure."

Maggie giggled. "Anything else?"

"Yeah, I'm giving up chocolate." In truth, giving up chocolate would be much harder than learning to live life more conservatively.

Ever since she was a kid, stifled by the restraints of her oh-so-proper Grosse Pointe family, she'd done everything she could to make her life more exciting. Her mother had prepared her for a life as an upper-class housewife. She'd been expected to find a husband and join the Junior League and sit on all the most important committees in the Detroit area. Every day, she'd kiss her husband on the cheek and send him off to a well-paying job in the city. Her children would attend the same private school she had. And her life would be dull as day-old dishwater.

Isabelle had decided early on she wasn't cut out to live her mother's life. She wanted something more than Grosse Pointe could offer, so she'd taken a small inheritance from her grandmother and grabbed the first flight to Chicago. Though the Channings were wealthy, they weren't so wealthy their influence extended beyond the environs of Detroit. She didn't have any trouble at all losing herself in the Windy City, building a new life for herself as a regular person with a regular job.

As she stared out at the dance floor, Isabelle had to smile. Her mother would probably hyperventilate if she knew her daughter was attending a society party with so many wealthy and eligible men. But Isabelle had vowed she would never marry for money, only for an all-consuming passion.

"Did you come with Luke?" Maggie asked.

She shook her head. "He was supposed to bring me, but he's off to some war zone tomorrow. He had to pack and pick up his airline tickets. He said he'd try to make it."

"I take it things aren't going too well with you two?"

"I think I make him crazy," Isabelle replied after taking a long sip of her champagne. "We have an occasional date but I know he sees other women. Of course, I haven't mentioned I see other men. Neither one of us is looking for a commitment." Isabelle sighed. "So what resolutions did you make?" she asked, her gaze fixed on a handsome man across the room. They made eye contact and Isabelle gave him a little wave and a coy smile. He looked kissable. She'd have to keep him in mind for later. "You're never without one of your plans."

"I've resolved to be blissfully happy."

Isabelle's gaze moved from the man to a small table in an alcove. "Look!" she cried, clutching Maggie's arm. "Old Eunice has hired a fortune-teller. Such a radical choice for a Spencer affair! Let's go find out what the next century holds for us."

Maggie shook her head. "I already know," she murmured.

"How can you possibly know?"

Maggie held out a trembling hand. A huge diamond twinkled beneath the soft light from the chandeliers. Isabelle felt her breath stop in her throat and she blinked.

"He asked me to marry him on Christmas Eve," Maggie explained. "I—I said yes. We're going to announce it right before midnight tonight."

Isabelle grabbed Maggie's hand in disbelief. It was definitely a diamond, big enough to be seen a block away. Geez, Maggie could signal planes with it if she ever had aspirations for a career in airport management. "No! But—but you can't marry him! He's such a—a bore, a stuffed shirt!" She crinkled her nose. "Besides, you don't love him."

A blush stained her friend's cheeks. "That's not true! I care about Colin and I respect him. And—and he can give me the life I want. A future and a real family."

"A family?" Isabelle asked. "His family? You want to be a—a pod person? A Stepford wife?"

"Colin and I will have a family of our own," she said softly. "We'll have children."

"Even if you don't love him?"

"My mother loved all her husbands and where did that get her? I'm not a passionate person, Is. I don't feel things the way you do. But that doesn't mean I can't be happy with Colin."

Isabelle sighed. "With a man you don't love?"

"I do love him!" Maggie cried. "Just because I don't dress up in Saran Wrap or dance naked on the kitchen table or send him my underwear in the mail, doesn't mean I don't love him."

Isabelle felt her own blush warm her cheeks. She knew Colin didn't approve of her behavior, but she'd never thought Maggie felt the same way. "I didn't mail my underwear. I sent it Federal Express."

"And what if I don't marry him? Is someone else going to come along? No one else is coming," Maggie said with a shake of her head. "Colin is the one. If I can't be happy with him, then I'll never be happy."

Isabelle shook her own head. How could Maggie possibly marry a man she didn't love? And not just any man, but Colin Spencer! Isabelle knew the expectations that came along with money. She'd lived them her entire life, until she'd walked away from Grosse Pointe. "You deserve so much better. You deserve fireworks and brass bands and—"

"I don't need those things." Maggie turned her gaze away. "I have everything I could possibly want. I promise."

There was nothing she could say to dissuade her. Maggie had made up her mind. Isabelle could only pray that over time, Maggie would realize what a mistake she'd made. Besides, they weren't getting married tomorrow. Isabelle would have plenty of time to make Maggie see the light. "Come on," she said, giving her a hug. "You might know what the future holds, but I don't. Let's go see that fortune-teller."

She shouldn't have been surprised by Maggie's decision, she mused as they crossed the ballroom. When Isabelle needed a good dose of common sense, she turned to Maggie Kelley. And when Maggie needed a shot of unbridled sentiment, she came to Isabelle. That's what made them such good friends, one lived by her head and the other by her heart.

Either way, a woman should feel passion for the man she was about to marry and all Maggie felt was admiration…and respect…and mild affection. Isabelle would never even consider marriage unless she was positively hot for a guy—not that she'd ever found a guy who held her interest for more than a few months.

Isabelle sighed. This could be a disaster in the making! And if she wasn't careful, she would be the one left on the outside. Colin Spencer was a powerful and persuasive man. But Isabelle Channing could be a formidable opponent, too. She'd have to come up with a clever plan to save her friend from a life of misery with that stuffy old stick. But first she'd have to study the enemy at close range, gather information about his past, prepare ammunition to be used against him.

By the end of the evening, she'd know what she was up against and she'd be ready to go to war.

THE MIDNIGHT HOUR was fast approaching and, to Isabelle's relief, Luke Fitzpatrick had finally arrived at the party. It hadn't taken him long to find her on the dance floor and interrupt her dance with a perfectly kissable investment banker whose girlfriend had decided she wanted a new man for the millennium.

Though Luke wasn't dressed in a tux, he was definitely the most intriguing man at the party. His dark hair was just a little too long to be considered fashionable and he wore a leather jacket and jeans, as if he was deliberately flouting the black-tie dress code.

She teased him for a while from the dance floor, watching his reaction to her silly flirtation with the banker, then reluctantly said goodbye to her dance partner and followed Luke off the floor. The champagne was just starting to make her feel warm all over and she grabbed another glass from a waiter's tray and sipped at it, batting her eyes at Luke over the rim of the crystal flute.

"We have something big to celebrate tonight," Isabelle said, trying to cajole him out of the dark mood he'd brought along. Luke was not the party type. He was more the mortars and missiles type, a guy who preferred a muddy battlefield to a fancy society soiree. His job as an international journalist made him quite the dashing figure, but like Colin Spencer, he was obsessed with his work.

Luke gave her a sideways glance. "And what's that?"

She smiled and took another sip of champagne, then arched her eyebrow in mock innocence. "Didn't you hear? My very best friend is going to marry your very best friend!"

"What did you say?" he gasped.

His reaction was instant and intense. Luke hadn't heard the big news and from the expression on his face, he wasn't at all pleased. Isabelle had always suspected he'd harbored more than platonic feelings for Maggie Kelley. After all, how could the two of them spend years in each other's company without ever giving in to curiosity?

She turned away and stared out at the dance floor, twirling the stem of her champagne flute between her fingers. "Don't look so surprised. They're announcing their engagement at midnight. You must have known it was coming. After all, you put the two of them together."

"Maggie is engaged to Colin?"

"Since Christmas Eve. But it'll be official tonight." She glanced down at her watch, then held her wrist out to him. "We still have time to stop it."

Isabelle met his gaze directly, curious to gauge the depth of his feelings. It wasn't as if it had come out of the blue. She'd seen the clues along the way. Whenever Luke looked at Maggie, his features softened and his eyes lingered just a bit too long. And though it wasn't obvious to the casual observer, Isabelle had noticed that Maggie always came first in his mind and in his heart. "You want to stop it, don't you?"

"Damn it," Luke muttered. "Why didn't she tell me?"

"I take it you don't approve?" Isabelle asked.

He opened his mouth to reply, then slowly pressed his lips together. "If—if Maggie is happy, then I'm happy for her."

Oh, he appeared so cool, but Isabelle could see the news had shaken him badly. "Happy? Are you sure about that?" she asked.

He sighed, then turned away from her, searching the dance floor. "Have you seen her?"

Isabelle backed away from him. She should have felt at least a twinge of jealousy, but she didn't. All she could feel was frustration. What the hell was

Maggie doing marrying a man she didn't love, when here stood a man who adored her? How could people be so stupid to ignore such profound feelings? "I think she went down to Colin's apartment," Isabelle murmured. "Why don't you go and find her? I'm sure you two have a lot to talk about."

With that, Luke nodded and headed for the door. A quiet oath slipped from Isabelle's lips and she turned away, searching for the nearest waiter. When she found him, she grabbed two glasses of champagne and downed them in short order.

This was exactly why she didn't have many friends! The responsibilities of making sure they were happy were just too much to bear. If she tried to convince Maggie to dump Colin, she'd alienate her best friend. And if she tried to force Luke into recognizing his true feelings, Colin would probably take out a contract on her life. But Isabelle couldn't stand back and watch as everyone made a mess of their lives.

The millennium was supposed to signify a fresh start, new beginnings and unparalleled possibilities. If everyone else was going to ignore the significance of this night, Isabelle was going to have to press the issue. She hitched up her gown and made a quick circle of the dance floor. If she expected to set everyone straight, she'd have to get to work right away. And then maybe she'd have just enough time to continue her search for the perfect midnight kiss.

2

COLIN WAS STILL ENGROSSED in conversation with the same group of men when Isabelle passed by. She'd searched the entire ballroom twice over, from band to bar to buffet table, looking for Maggie. But Colin's fiancée hadn't yet returned to the party. Then again, Isabelle mused, Luke had also disappeared. She considered taking a trip down to Colin's apartment, but decided it would be better to sit back and let events unfold.

If Luke really did love Maggie, he'd have to confess his feelings sooner or later. What better time than on the eve of the millennium when all were forced to reevaluate their lives. Luke might even be pouring out his heart at this very minute, Isabelle mused.

Life was too short for caution and discretion, she decided. She was Maggie's friend and it was time to take action. Smoothing back an errant strand of hair, Isabelle slowly approached the men, a coy smile touching her lips when Colin turned to look at her. "Colin," she cried. "You promised me a dance and I simply won't let you back out on your promises."

She didn't give him a moment to refuse, for she was certain he'd find some charming way to weasel out of a waltz with her. A sweet smile and a demure apology satisfied the rest of the group and she slipped her arm through his and pulled him toward the dance floor. They'd only managed a few steps before he stopped.

"What are you up to, Isabelle?"

She gave his arm a tug, but he refused to move any farther. "I thought we might have a dance. It's New Year's Eve. You seem to have misplaced Maggie and I can't find Luke." She feigned a frown. "You don't suppose they're together, do you? Perhaps we should go look for them."

"I just talked to Luke a little while ago." He paused, then fixed her with an aggravated glare. "You told him about the engagement."

Isabelle smiled smugly. "Why, yes, I believe it did come up in conversation. And did he offer his congratulations?"

Colin's jaw went tight. Even tension didn't alter his perfect profile. Isabelle's gaze skimmed his face and she fought the urge to reach out and run her thumb along his lower lip. She'd always thought he had an unremarkable mouth, stern and unyielding. But at close range, it wasn't that way at all. His mouth was quite extraordinary. Very…kissable.

"I think he was insulted that Maggie hadn't told him first," Colin replied, staring out at the crowd. "He dragged me onto the terrace and chewed me out. He expected me to ask permission. But then, you knew he wouldn't be thrilled when you told him, didn't you?"

"I was just conveying a bit of happy news," she said in mock innocence. "It is happy news, isn't it?"

"Yes, it is," he muttered. "Though it's a little irritating no one else shares my opinion. Neither you nor Fitzpatrick nor my parents."

"Hmm. Well, that's a problem, isn't it." She shrugged. "Let's dance."

He stared at her with a suspicious glint in his eye and she thought he'd refuse her on the spot. "Isabelle, why pretend we like each other? I think it's a rather inefficient use of our energies. You're Maggie's friend and I have to respect that. But I don't have to enjoy your company. If you just keep your distance, we'll get along fine."

Isabelle reached out and flicked an imaginary speck of lint from his lapel, her eyes lowered flirtatiously. "Good grief, you are a snooty britches, aren't you," she said, her words dripping with acid.

He blinked in surprise, as if he was insulted by her astute observation. "I am not a—a snooty britches." Colin grabbed her elbow and pulled her toward the dance floor. "Let's get this over with," he muttered.

"Charming," she replied. "I hope this isn't how you swept Maggie off her feet."

Colin slipped his arm around her waist and splayed out his fingers in the small of her back. For a moment, her attention was drawn to the warmth that seeped through her gown, the gentle strength of his hand on her body, the control he seemed to snatch from her by a mere touch. He pulled her close, much closer than she expected, and she held her breath.

She wanted him at arm's length, but instead, their hips brushed as they fell into step. He moved with astounding grace for such an uptight man. He held her just firmly enough so she could anticipate his next move, a turn to the left, a change of direction, and before long they were cutting a rather impressive rug. She gave silent thanks to her mother who'd insisted on ballroom-dancing lessons when Isabelle was nine years old.

"You're very good," she murmured, unable to think of anything else to say.

"So are you," he admitted grudgingly.

"Miss Peabody's School of Dance," she said. "Every Saturday morning for two years. You should see me rumba. I'm a wild woman."

Colin chuckled dryly, his stony facade cracking for a moment. "For me it was cotillions at the country club. I can still feel that itchy wool suit. I couldn't scratch with those gloves on and the bow tie nearly choked me." He glanced at her. "Cotillions are a kind of formal ball," he said, obviously thinking he had to explain. "All the kids had to go." He paused. "Not all the kids...I mean, just..."

"Rich kids?" Isabelle shook her head and sighed. "You really are a snooty britches." With that, she turned her head away and refused to talk to him anymore. Now *she* felt insulted, though she wasn't sure why. She'd never told anyone about her background, and when friends assumed she'd come from a working-class family, she hadn't bothered to correct them. In truth, Isabelle had left her wealthy family far behind and, though her parents might look at her life as a step down the social ladder, Isabelle considered it a step up.

She was working-class now and proud of it. She lived in a tiny apartment and ate tuna twice a week. She hauled her laundry to the Laundromat and took the bus because she couldn't afford a car. She worked at a job she loved, but that barely paid enough to live on. And when the bills piled up and the money was tight, she never even considered calling home for help. Isabelle Channing was a completely independent woman and that's exactly the way she wanted it. Unlike Maggie, she didn't want a man running her life.

"I'm sorry," Colin murmured.

Isabelle turned her face toward him. Her breath caught in her throat as she realized how close he was. His chin grazed her temple almost like a caress. For a moment, their gazes locked and Isabelle felt an odd detachment, as if her brain had suddenly shut down. She forgot he was Maggie's fiancé and she looked at him without regard for the man she knew him to be.

They might have met on the sidewalk or glanced at each other across a crowded restaurant. Isabelle knew that had they been strangers, she would have been attracted to him. There was something about him, the appearance of total control masking a simmering masculinity just waiting to be ignited.

The current of attraction racing through her caused her to stumble, so taken aback was she by the intensity. She stepped on his toe and her foot twisted off the heel of her shoe. With a soft cry, Isabelle felt herself falling. But then Colin's hands grasped her waist and righted her without missing a step.

"Are you all right?" he asked.

Isabelle felt her cheeks grow hot. "I—I'm fine."

"Too much champagne?"

"Yes," she said, taking up the excuse with a grateful smile. She tried to focus on her feet rather than the effect his handsome face had on her senses. Silently, she counted out the steps of the waltz, but before it was over, she'd managed to trample on his toes at least three more times.

When the band finally brought the music to a conclusion, Isabelle was ready to get out of Colin Spencer's arms. His touch had a disturbing effect on her, as if she found some pleasure in it. But she detested Colin Spencer! He was everything she disliked in a man—arrogant, condescending, domineering. There were times she'd just as soon slap his face than contemplate how handsome it was.

Besides, if she expected to throw a wrench into this ill-conceived engagement between Maggie and Colin, she'd have to keep her wits about her. Mooning over him at every turn would not help matters. "Thank you for the dance, Colin."

He nodded. "My pleasure, Isabelle."

They stood on the dance floor for a long moment, staring at each other, as if they thought they ought to hurl some insult or snide remark. Isabelle swallowed hard, unable to take her eyes off him, seeing for the first time a hint of the man Colin Spencer really was. But when the band started up again, party guests danced around them, jostling them both. Finally, Colin took her hand and escorted her off the dance floor.

When they reached the safety of the crowd, Isabelle pulled her fingers from his and rubbed her hands together. "Perhaps, I'll visit the buffet table," she said lamely.

"And I should get back to my guests." He glanced over her shoulder and stared blankly into the crowd. "If you see Maggie, tell her I'd like to speak to her."

Isabelle nodded, then watched as Colin rejoined the group of gentlemen he'd been speaking with before she'd dragged him away. With a soft oath, Isabelle gathered her skirt in her fists and turned to hurry out of the ballroom. Why was she so bothered—and so fascinated—with Colin Spencer? She'd never lost her composure with a man. Why him? Isabelle pressed her palm to her forehead. Maybe she had drunk too much champagne. Or maybe it was the atmosphere, the excitement surrounding the approaching hour of midnight.

"The pole shift," Isabelle murmured. It must be the pole shift! All the prophecies had warned of a giant magnetic storm as the millennium passed, with the two poles of the earth switching gravitational power between. The earth would shudder and everything would be thrown amiss. Though Isabelle didn't believe in such a silly notion, there could be something to it. That's what could be causing all this chaos in her brain. "Stray magnetic waves," she said.

She caught sight of Madame Blavatka plying her trade at the small table on the far side of the dance floor. Perhaps the psychic could offer some advice for resisting this strange phenomenon. She seemed to know more about these prophecies than anyone else at the party.

Isabelle grabbed another glass of champagne from a waiter and downed it in one long gulp. If she was going to hear her future, she'd need fortification. She took a deep breath and set off across the ballroom, determined to find out what the new millennium would hold for her. And even more determined to leave this strange attraction to her friend's fiancé in the old millennium!

ISABELLE STOOD at the elevators and pushed the down button over and over again, tapping her foot impatiently as she waited. Eunice Spencer's big bash had turned into the worst party she'd ever attended.

She'd lost track of Luke, Maggie was nowhere to be found, and she was afraid to get within ten feet of Colin. She'd spent the past half hour wandering around the ballroom, engaging in idle flirtations and wondering why she'd even agreed to come. If she were smart, which she'd just resolved to be for the new year, she'd ride the elevator to the street level, grab a cab and go home to toast the new millennium on her own. But she had to find Maggie before she left.

The psychic had had nothing of interest to tell her, except that Isabelle would do well to think before she acted. Madame Blavatka was probably still stinging from Isabelle's earlier skepticism regarding her talents as she read Maggie's fortune. The fortune-teller had also told her she'd kiss a tall, dark man at midnight. Unless her cabdriver wanted a quick smooch, Isabelle was sure *that* prediction wasn't going to come true.

As she stepped onto the elevator, she readjusted her wrap over a cold bottle of champagne she'd filched for her own little celebration. Her thoughts drifted back to the fortune-teller's prophecy for Maggie. Maggie had been so reluctant to hear what the future held, but Madame Blavatka had only confirmed what Maggie wanted to hear: she belonged with Colin. But it was so clear to Isabelle that Maggie didn't love him!

"What a tangle," Isabelle murmured. If Luke did secretly love Maggie, then why had he introduced her to Colin? She considered that question for a long moment, not coming up with a logical answer. And if Maggie loved Luke, why had she insisted he date

Isabelle? It seemed the two of them had been working at cross-purposes all along.

A slow realization dawned and Isabelle smiled. Oh, the games people played in the name of love. She had played so many herself, she recognized the strategy immediately. Luke had introduced Maggie to Colin in an attempt to force her feelings to the surface. And Maggie had set Isabelle up with Luke to do the same thing! Jealousy provided powerful motivation. But not so powerful in this case, Isabelle mused. Maggie had taken the little game too far when she agreed to marry Colin.

Isabelle took a quick sip of champagne out of the open bottle, anticipating the fireworks she was about to set off. Now that she had figured all the players out, maybe she could have a part in the game. She'd just tell Maggie of her suspicions about Luke. And she'd make sure her friend ended up with the right man by the end of the night.

She punched the button for the forty-eighth floor, praying she'd find Maggie alone in Colin's apartment. It was the only place she could possibly be—unless she had already run away with Luke, a remote prospect at best. When the doors opened in front of Isabelle, she looked up to find Colin Spencer waiting in the hallway outside his apartment. His smile faded slightly and Isabelle could tell he wasn't pleased to see her again. "Isabelle." His greeting couldn't have been more unenthusiastic.

"Colin," Isabelle murmured. "It's nearly midnight. What are you doing down here while all those important guests are upstairs?"

"I came down to find Maggie."

Isabelle poked her head out of the elevator and looked around. "Where is she?"

"She wasn't in the apartment. I must have missed her."

Isabelle smiled. "Maybe she's reconsidered your proposal and run off. I hear the circus is in town."

He stepped inside the elevator and braced his shoulder against the wall, watching her casually. Isabelle ground her teeth. Good grief, the man even leaned sexy! Had he asked *her* to marry him, she might have even slipped into a moment of insanity and agreed. How could she possibly fault Maggie for doing the same? He was like a perfect Greek statue, cool and polished—and he looked delicious in a tuxedo. Her mind wandered for a moment as she considered what he might look like *out* of his tuxedo, but Isabelle pushed such inappropriate thoughts aside with a silent curse.

"I guess that's what you get for ignoring her. Going up?" Isabelle asked in a nonchalant voice.

He nodded, then continued to smile at her, his sculpted mouth turned up just slightly at the corners in a sardonic smirk. Isabelle reached over to the control buttons to push the penthouse level again, but a sudden impulse struck her. She took her finger and ran it down one row of buttons on the control panel and then the other, until she'd lit up every floor beneath Colin's apartment.

The doors closed and she turned back to him, a mischievous smile curling her lips. "I'm going down. Floor by floor. You can take a little ride with me and we can talk."

He stepped around her to look at the control panel

and his smile faded. "I have to get back upstairs, Isabelle. I don't have time for your silly games."

She took another gulp of champagne and held the bottle out to him.

He shook his head. "I don't drink. I never have."

Isabelle sighed dramatically. "Oh, relax," she said. "We'll be there in time. I wouldn't want you to miss the big announcement."

His eyes narrowed. "I find that hard to believe. I get the feeling you don't approve of our plans."

"Where would you get that idea? I'm Maggie's best friend. And as her best friend, I think it's my responsibility to make sure your intentions are... honorable." Isabelle grabbed her skirt, drew it up to her knees and sat down on the floor of the elevator. She patted a spot beside her. "Come on, Colin. Take a load off. We'll have a nice little talk and get to know each other better."

The elevator bumped to a stop on the forty-seventh floor and the doors opened, then closed. For a moment, Isabelle thought Colin might take the opportunity to get out. But he shrugged, and slowly sat down beside her. With a sigh, he grabbed the proffered bottle of champagne and took a long swallow, wincing at the taste. "All right. What do you want to know?"

Isabelle tipped her head back and rested it against the wall. "I'll get right to the point. How did you know you were in love with Maggie?"

His eyebrow arched and he sent her a cool look. "Don't you think that subject is a little personal?"

Isabelle reached over and slipped her arm through his, bumping playfully against his shoulder. But touching him was far less casual than she expected and she felt a shiver run down her spine. "Indulge me," she said, trying to control the slight tremor in her voice. "I've never been in love in my life. At least I don't think I have. Give me some insight."

Colin considered her question for a long moment as the doors opened and closed again. He took another swallow of champagne. "I'm not sure I can give you an answer."

"And why not? Come on, Colin. Loosen the laces on your corset and kick back. We're all friends here."

He scratched idly at the label on the bottle. She could almost hear him formulating his reply, carefully choosing the proper words as if he were presenting a business strategy. "Well, there are so many factors that come into play. Maggie is sweet and…and agreeable. And she's pretty. I know she'll make a wonderful mother."

Isabelle laughed out loud. "Sounds like you're describing a farm animal."

He shot her an aggravated look. "I guess I'm not very good with words."

"Oh, but you convinced Maggie to marry you. You must be good with a few words." Or maybe he was simply good in bed, Isabelle mused. For a man she had once considered unappealing, Colin was proving to be just the opposite. Every time he looked at her, she found herself softening under his considerable charms.

"What is it you want, Isabelle?" he asked in an irritated voice.

She carefully straightened her skirt, plucking at the bugle beads that circled the hem. "I want to know if you love Maggie Kelley. And I don't want you to just say the words. I want to know if she's the

most important thing in your life. If you'll do anything in your power to make her happy. If you'd give
up everything you have and everything you are to be
with her."

This time he laughed out loud. "Don't be ridiculous. Why would I have to give everything up?"

"Do you love her? Answer the question."

"Of course," Colin said. "Now can we change the
subject?"

"Say it," Isabelle demanded. "Say the words and
look right into my eyes. Because I'll know if you're
lying."

He stared at her, anger flickering across his expression. The door opened and shut again and he pushed
to his feet. Isabelle was certain he'd get out, and
when the doors opened he almost did. But then he
stopped and turned back to her. With a long sigh, he
ran his fingers through his hair and braced his arm
on the wall above her head.

And when his eyes finally met hers, she knew the
truth as clearly as she knew the truth of Maggie's
feelings. He looked so vulnerable, so utterly miserable, that Isabelle regretted pushing him so far. "You
don't, do you," she murmured, staring up at him.
"Don't bother to lie, Colin, because this is serious. If
you lie about this, lightning will strike you dead and
you'll go straight to hell."

At that instant, the elevator jerked to a stop and the
lights flickered once, then went off completely. For a
moment, there was nothing but silence and impenetrable darkness. Then Isabelle cried out and scrambled to her feet, feeling her way in the dark until she
ran up against Colin's tall, lean body. She felt his

hands circle her waist as he steadied her, pulling her hard against him.

"Well, if lightning has struck and I'm headed down," Colin said, his voice coming at her out of the blackness, "I guess you're coming with me."

COLIN KNEW they weren't in any danger. Not even close. But it felt good to give Isabelle Channing a taste of her own medicine. Good Lord, the woman could twist a conversation into so many knots a guy would say anything just to get her to shut up. How did Luke ever stand her? She had to be a real pain to have around.

Then again, she was gorgeous. Colin suspected her beauty and her passionate nature made all her other flaws fade. He'd always found Isabelle infinitely intriguing, but that was as far as it went. He couldn't possibly justify an attraction to a woman as wild and willful as she was. Maggie was much more suited to his own character.

At least one good thing had come from the dark elevator, he mused. Isabelle had stopped her inquisition. Colin squinted in the darkness and tried to make out the control panel. If his guess was right, the elevators in the Spencer Center had just been hit with the millennium bug. Though the maintenance department had done everything possible to minimize potential problems, the entire building was run by computer—the heat, the air-conditioning, the lights, even the window-washing system. After eight at night, the elevators ran on a timed program, the computer recording every stop of every car, twenty-four hours a day.

"What's going on?" Isabelle asked, her hands clutching at his forearms. "What happened?"

He gently rubbed the small of her back in an attempt to calm her. "The system went down."

"Down? Down?" Her voice took on an hysterical edge. "Don't say that word while we're hanging by a skinny little rope, thousands of feet above the ground!"

She pressed against him and Colin could feel the soft swell of her breasts through the fabric of his shirt, teasing at his imagination. The scent of her perfume touched his nose, exotic and a bit spicy, working like a drug on his senses. Clenching his teeth, he pushed her back and gave her a gentle shake. "Calm down. The power went out. The millennium bug must have hit the elevator system a little early. And we're not hanging by a rope, but a steel cable. And we're no more than seven hundred feet aboveground."

"Oh, just seven hundred?" Isabelle scoffed. "Well, we can certainly survive a fall of seven hundred feet. For a moment there, I was worried."

Colin couldn't help but chuckle. She really was amusing at times, when she wasn't sexy as hell. "The generators will kick in in a few moments and then the maintenance staff will reboot the computer and we'll be out of here in no time." He paused. "You know, this is all your fault. If we had gone directly up to the reception, we wouldn't be stuck here."

"Oh, don't blame me. You were the one tempting fate by lying."

"I didn't lie," Colin said.

The emergency lights flickered and then illuminated the inside of the elevator with a dim glow.

Colin looked down at Isabelle to find her wrapped in his arms, her face pressed against his shoulder. She glanced up at him. A blush crept up her cheeks and she slowly untangled herself from his embrace.

Colin fought a satisfied smile. He couldn't ever recall seeing Isabelle Channing blush. She wasn't prone to embarrassment. "Don't worry," he said, "I won't mention your...indiscretion to Maggie."

She gave him an acidic glare, then retreated to the far side of the elevator. "Why aren't we moving?"

"Give it time," he replied, taking a spot on the opposite wall.

They waited in uneasy silence for nearly five minutes, regarding each other warily. But the car didn't move. Isabelle stepped to the control panel and started to punch the buttons. "Isn't there a phone in here? Can't we call for help? There must be an alarm."

"It's all done by computer. They know we're in here because the computer senses the weight of the car."

Isabelle sighed and sat back down on the floor. He could tell she was frightened and too proud to show it. Colin grudgingly took a place beside her and grabbed the champagne bottle from the floor. He held it out and Isabelle took a sip before he took another healthy swig. He didn't care for alcohol, but he was starting to enjoy champagne. The more he drank, the more relaxed he became. And considering all his carefully laid plans were slowly blowing up in front of his face, he definitely needed to relax.

"I guess the announcement is off," Isabelle said. "It's just a few minutes until midnight and you can't get to the reception."

Colin shrugged. "Maggie will be disappointed. And my parents, well, I don't even want to think about what they're going to say."

"And what about you?" Isabelle asked.

"We'll make the announcement another—"

"No," Isabelle insisted. "Tell me how you really feel."

He smiled ruefully and slowly shook his head. He knew exactly how he felt, but he wasn't about to admit it to Maggie's best friend. This engagement had to go forward. There was too much depending on it.

"Tell me," Isabelle urged. "Anything said in this elevator stays here. I swear."

Colin knew he should keep his feelings to himself. But the champagne had loosened his tongue. And for once, he was glad to have someone who was at least interested in *his* feelings. "It sounds bad," he began, "but, in all honesty, I feel like I just dodged a bullet." He sighed and raked his fingers through his hair, bracing his elbows on his knees. "Hell, I'm really an ass. I don't know how I stand myself."

"You are an ass."

He sent her a sideways glance. "Thank you. I think that's the first time we've ever agreed on anything." Colin raised the champagne bottle again, then wiped his mouth with the back of his hand. "Ever since I graduated from college, there's been this subtle pressure for me to settle down. I'm the only son and my family is depending on me to carry on the Spencer line. Talk about feeling like a farm animal. You're looking at the Spencer stud pony."

"So you decided to marry Maggie?"

He shrugged. "It was time. If I didn't do something, my father was going to disinherit me. Then where would I be? No job, no money, no place to live."

"How could you do that to Maggie?"

"Don't you realize what I can offer her? She's wanted a real family her entire life. She'll have a beautiful home, perfect children, anything her heart desires."

"Except the love of her husband."

"What is the big deal about love? We care about each other, isn't that enough? Hell, my parents certainly didn't marry for love and they've been married nearly forty years. My mother married my father because he could give her the kind of life she wanted."

"Like father, like son, that's your excuse?" Isabelle shook her head. "Look at your father, Colin. Is that the kind of life you want? Working sixty or seventy hours a week, the same job, the same desk, every day for the rest of your life?"

"I'm a Spencer. I don't get the life I want, I get the life I was born into."

"If you weren't a Spencer, what would you do? It's the eve of a whole new millennium. You have the chance to change your life. What would you wish for?"

"Unfathomable wealth and absolute power."

"Anything," Isabelle repeated. "Besides that."

Colin sat back and thought about it for a while, then grinned. "I've always wanted to go to Vegas and gamble. I've never gambled. I'd like to see what it feels like to just throw money away. To risk a bundle on the turn of a card or the toss of the dice."

"You *can* do anything you want," Isabelle reminded him. "It is your life."

"No, I can't. I'm not you, Isabelle. I have responsibilities and I take those responsibilities seriously."

Isabelle turned to him, grabbed his hands and squeezed tightly. "You can. It doesn't take courage, it just takes one step and then another and then another. Toss your fate to the wind."

He glanced around, and smiled. "There's no wind in here."

"When this elevator starts, if we go up, you go back to the reception and announce your engagement. And if we go down, you go to Las Vegas. Take a chance, Spencer. You've always wanted to gamble, why not start now?"

Colin raised the champagne bottle to his lips, then noticed it was empty. He set it down beside him. He wasn't sure whether it was the alcohol or the beautiful woman sitting next to him, but he considered the notion for a long moment, then nodded. "All right," he said. "If we go down, we go to Vegas. If we go up, I marry Maggie."

Just then, an alarm sounded and the elevator jerked again. Isabelle scrambled to her feet and watched the panel above the door. Even though the car was moving, the lights weren't. Colin wasn't sure whether they were going up or down. He slowly stood and awaited his fate, knowing if the elevator ended up in the lobby, he could just ride it back up to the top floor.

Let Isabelle believe he was going along with her. Hell, he wanted to believe it, too, at least for a little while. He was sick and tired of analyzing every move he made. Isabelle was right, he was turning into his father. And if he looked honestly at his life, he hadn't done anything spontaneous since...since he had ordered a red BMW instead of a black one. And even then, he'd decided red was too flashy and traded it for black.

Isabelle glanced over at him, her eyes wide. "It feels like we're going down."

"It feels like up to me."

The elevator bumped to a stop and they both held their breaths as the doors slowly slid open.

3

HE FELT AS IF he'd been hit by a truck. And then the truck had stopped and backed over his head once or twice for good measure. Colin slowly opened one eye and then the other, moaning softly as the searing light of day shot through his brain and burned a hole in the back of his head. His mouth was as dry as a desert and every bone in his body ached. He focused his gaze on the ceiling only to find his own miserable reflection staring back at him from a huge mirror.

Colin flung out his arms to stop the spinning of the bed, then realized the bed *was* actually moving—very slowly. He carefully reached out for the edge, determined to get off before his stomach could protest anymore. As he inched his way to one side, he encountered only endless mattress. With a long moan, he pushed himself up on one elbow to find he was sleeping in the center of a round bed the size of a small swimming pool.

Across the room, a whirlpool, the size of a large bed, bubbled and steamed. Besides the bed and whirlpool, the room included a wall full of video and audio equipment, a complete sitting area, floor-to-ceiling windows, a fountain and glass-block wall he guessed hid the bathroom. All in all, a study in architectural excess.

He fixed his gaze on the glass wall, wondering if

he could make it to the bathroom without passing out. Not willing to risk it, Colin tried to gather his thoughts and regain his equilibrium. He knew he was in Las Vegas, he remembered that much. And he vaguely recalled coming here with Isabelle Channing on the company jet. With a wince, he also remembered the mess he'd left behind—Maggie, the engagement, his parents and a shamble he used to call his life. Considering the state of his head, he decided to think about those matters at a later time, after he'd survived this hangover.

Beyond that, everything was a dim blur punctuated by only a few brief moments of lucidity. His feeble attempt at clearing his head was brought to an abrupt stop when he noticed a figure moving behind the glass-block wall. The silhouette was unfocused but he could tell it was a woman—a naked woman!

She slowly bent over at the waist, her hair tumbling forward. Then she twisted a towel around her head and straightened, her slender arms raised above her shoulders. Colin's eyes drifted along the line of her body, her breasts and her narrow waist, the lush curves of her hips and backside. He felt as though he'd wandered into some high-class peep show, watching as she dried her body one exquisite limb at a time. A thread of desire snaked through him and he recognized the sure signs of arousal.

The show didn't end there, for after she was dry, she smoothed every inch of her body with her palms. Colin could only guess she was applying some type of lotion. His fingers twitched as he tried to recall touching her. Had he skimmed his palms over those same spots—the inside of her thigh, the small of her back, the nape of her neck? He wanted to remember, but no matter how hard he tried, he couldn't.

When she finally pulled a bathrobe over her naked form, Colin grabbed a pillow and placed it strategically on his lap, then waited to see who he'd spent the night with. Good Lord, he'd never once slept with a complete stranger. He scrambled to remember a name, a face, but as the woman emerged from behind the wall, he realized the worst. He already knew her name—and that face was unforgettable.

"Isabelle!"

The towel slipped off her head and she reached up and grabbed it, then let it drop to the floor. "You're awake!" she said with a smile. She crossed the room and plopped down on the end of the bed, tucking her legs beneath her and drying her damp hair. "I thought you'd sleep the rest of the day away. You drifted off right about the same time the sun was coming up."

Colin's gaze dropped to the neck of her plush bathrobe, the fabric gaping to reveal the tempting curves of her breasts. His mind raced and another flood of desire pooled in the vicinity of his lap. He was in a hotel room in Las Vegas with Isabelle Channing. He'd been ogling her like some sex-starved pervert. And she still was naked beneath that bathrobe!

"How are you feeling?" she asked. "You look like you were hit by a truck. Champagne will do that."

"Wh—what are you doing here?"

"In Las Vegas?" Isabelle asked with a frown. "Don't you remember? We flew here on your company jet. Right after we skipped out on your mother's party and your engagement."

"Of course I remember," Colin said, rubbing his temples. "I—I remember the elevator and the bottle of champagne and the limo ride to Meigs Field. And I remember gambling. I meant, what are you doing *here*, in this room?"

"I was taking a shower. You should try the whirlpool," she said. "It's so relaxing. I bet it would help you get rid of your headache. I assume you have a headache. Or do you always look so constipated in the morning? Champagne will do that, too."

Colin cleared his throat. "Did you…I mean, did we…"

"Sleep together?" Isabelle asked. She nodded. "We spent the night in the same bed, if that's what you're asking. I wonder where they get sheets for a bed this shape?"

"And did we…"

She stared at him for a long moment, then realized what he was really asking. "*Sleep* together?" This time, she shrugged. "If you could call it that. You fell asleep as soon as you hit the pillow and you snored all night long. Champagne will—"

"Do that," Colin completed. "I get the picture." As he watched the scenery in the hotel room slowly pass by behind Isabelle, he closed his eyes to battle another wave of nausea. "Is there any way to stop the bed from moving?"

He felt her weight shift and then suddenly she was on top of him, her body pressed along the length of his. Her robe parted in the front and he could feel the soft flesh of her breasts pressing against his chest, the hard nubs of her nipples skimming his skin. Colin's eyes snapped open. Her lips were just inches from his. "What the hell are you—"

"The controls are over here on the headboard," Isabelle explained, stretching her arm out above his ear. He held his breath and tried to ignore what was going on below his waist. Thank goodness for the pillow, which now served as a barrier between them. And thank goodness he'd possessed enough will-power last night to resist Isabelle's tantalizing body, even though willpower was in short supply now.

She slid off him and he couldn't help but risk a glance. The robe had fallen open, revealing a provocative view of her naked body. But she didn't seem to be bothered with modesty. Isabelle casually tugged the robe closed and tightened the belt, before resuming her spot at the end of the bed.

Maybe he would do best to get his mind off Isabelle Channing's breasts and move on to more distracting subjects. "I remember gambling. So how much did I lose?"

Isabelle shrugged. "A lot. I lost track at thirty thousand."

He gasped. "Thirty thousand dollars? But I didn't have that much cash on me."

"You lost your cash on the first two hands of blackjack. But you had a credit card," she said. "We pretty much maxed that out. I thought a guy like you would carry a higher credit limit. Enough to buy a house or yacht or a fleet of fancy cars."

"I lost thirty thousand dollars," Colin repeated, stunned by the sheer magnitude of his stupidity—and his apparent lack of skill at gambling.

"But you won big at the craps table," Isabelle offered, patting him on the knee.

"I did?"

"About two hundred."

"Two hundred thousand?"

"No, just two hundred regular."

"How did we pay for this room?"

"We didn't. The suite belongs to someone named Ernie. He sat next to you at the blackjack table. He felt sorry for us and gave us the key. He'll be back at noon. Lucky for us, you lost big. There isn't a vacancy in town."

"Oh, God, what else did I do?" he asked, burying his face in his hands.

"Do you mean, did you dance on any tables with lamp shades on your head? Did you throw up in public? Did you come on to any married women at the baccarat table?"

He looked at her through his fingers, not certain he wanted to hear more of the truth. "Did I?"

"No, to the first two," Isabelle said. "You made a clumsy pass at a blonde, but then her husband threatened to kill you and he dragged her away."

"How did we get here?"

"We came up here after the wedding," she said.

Colin's stomach rolled and pitched and he braced his hands on either side of him, certain Las Vegas had just been hit by a major earthquake. The wedding? He certainly would have remembered attending a wedding last night! And who the hell did he know that was getting married in Vegas?

"Is the room still spinning?" Isabelle asked. "It's best if you close your eyes and take deep, even breaths. And try not to think about greasy food—fried chicken, steak burritos, bacon, stuff like that. That always makes me retch."

Colin ignored her advice. "The wedding," he said,

his voice deceptively calm. "Tell me about the wedding."

Isabelle frowned. "You don't remember? But that was the best part."

"Of course I do," Colin lied. "Just not all the details. Refresh my memory. Where was this wedding?"

"Just outside the hotel on Fremont Street. They have this huge canopy of lights and there was music."

He remembered the lights, laser sharp and bright with color. "There was a big crowd out on the street."

"Yes! They were trying to set a millennium record," Isabelle explained. "Two thousand weddings in twenty-four hours."

"And—and who got married?"

"We did," Isabelle said with a shrug.

Colin laughed out loud. Leave it to Isabelle. He should have expected this from her, just another attempt to shake him up with some audacious story. "No, really. Who got married?"

Isabelle gave him a long look, her eyes wide, her gaze searching. "We did." She scrambled off the bed and returned a moment later with a piece of paper. "It's all legal," she said, pushing it beneath his nose. "See, you signed right there. Groom, Colin Spencer. Bride, Isabelle Channing. We were number 1,282."

He squinted at the marriage license and his heart lurched when he saw the familiar handwriting under the heading Groom. Slowly, it all came back, bits and pieces, whims and impulses, all fueled by too much champagne. He *had* married Isabelle. They'd gone out for a walk after he lost all that money and had been swallowed up by the festivities outside the casino. He'd proposed as a joke, but then she'd teased him into going through with it. He never thought they were performing legal marriages! He thought it was just a big party. "But—but I'm engaged to Maggie," Colin said.

Isabelle smiled sweetly. "But you're married to me."

With a curse, Colin crushed the license in his fist, and threw the covers off. It was only then he realized he was stark naked beneath the sheets. Isabelle's eyebrow slowly rose as she took in the view, but he quickly snatched the sheet, yanked it from the bed and wrapped it around his waist. "I can't be married to you," he said, standing up on wobbly legs. For a moment, he thought he might keel over, but then the dizziness passed. "I—I'm going to marry Maggie."

"After what you did to her last night, I don't think she's going to be too anxious to marry you."

"That was all a mistake," he said. "A mistake I'm going to fix right now." He glanced around the room, his head pounding with every movement. "Where are my clothes? I need to get out of here. I'm going back to Chicago. I'll explain everything and she'll understand. I'm going to marry Maggie."

"Then that would be bigamy," Isabelle replied, studying him with a look of mock innocence, a look that made him want to throw her down on the bed and kiss the smirk right off her lips! Another memory flashed in his mind—warm mouths, probing tongues, jolts of overwhelming desire. "Oh, no," Colin murmured, closing his eyes. The images became clearer. He had kissed Isabelle Channing here in this bed. At least, he thought he had. He drew a deep breath and tried to marshal his thoughts. There had to be a way to get out of this. He couldn't possibly be married to Isabelle Channing!

"We'll have it annulled," he said. "I was drunk. I didn't know what I was doing. Any judge will see that."

"But you remember our wedding, don't you?"

"Well, yes," he replied. "But I was still drunk. Besides, we didn't consummate it."

"But we did," Isabelle said. "And I think if you do the deed, then the marriage becomes official."

"I asked if we slept together and you said no!" Surely he would have remembered that! Her tempting body, those perfect breasts, the sensation of losing himself inside of her as she arched beneath him in ecstasy.

Isabelle sighed impatiently. "You slept and I was awake for most of the night. That always happens after sex. I just get so wound up, I can't settle down."

"We—we had sex," he said.

"It wasn't great, if that's what you're getting at. Champagne will—"

"Do that!" he shouted. "I know. You don't need to say it again." His anger flared, but not at her obtuse behavior. Instead, he'd been insulted by her offhand commentary on his skills in the bedroom. He scolded himself inwardly. What did he care how he performed? He'd slept with Isabelle Channing, wasn't that bad enough?

"Damn it, Isabelle, just how much champagne did I drink? I'm a rational guy. I live my life by certain standards. I know what I'm capable of, drunk or sober. And I'm not capable of running off to Las Vegas, gambling away thirty thousand dollars and marrying someone I can barely tolerate. Now, I think it's time to call an end to this little practical joke of yours and admit that nothing happened."

"That would be a little hard to do," she said, pushing herself up off the bed. She brushed a kiss across his lips. "So, husband, we get a free breakfast with the room. Do you prefer eggs or French toast?"

Just the thought of food made Colin's stomach pitch. He groaned softly, then walked to the bathroom. "I'm going to take a shower. And when I get done, we're going to figure out how to make this all go away."

"Do you want me to come with you and scrub your back?" Isabelle called.

In truth, the offer was tempting. He'd like nothing more than to lose himself in mindless passion and numbing desire. But if he expected to make things right, he'd have to keep his wits about him. And it hadn't taken him long to realize that in the presence of Isabelle Channing, his wits were the first thing to go.

ROOM SERVICE ARRIVED in a half hour with their breakfast. Isabelle let the waiter in and he efficiently set up a variety of entrées on the dining table near the windows. The sound of the shower drifted out from the bathroom and Isabelle wondered how much longer Colin intended to stay in there. She was about to check to see if he'd fallen asleep when the running water stopped. A figure moved on the other side of the glass wall and she watched as she sipped a cup of hot coffee.

Though she could see he'd wrapped a towel around his waist, Isabelle didn't have to imagine what was beneath the damp terry-cloth. After he'd tossed aside the covers, her suspicions had been confirmed. Colin Spencer had an incredible body, a body any woman would find hard to resist. From his broad, smooth chest to his flat belly to his long muscular legs, Isabelle couldn't find a single feature that caused complaint. And as far as his manly equipment went, she could tell that was in fine working order as well…not that she'd had a chance to test it.

A tiny sliver of guilt shot through her. Maybe she shouldn't have lied to him. But as long as he didn't remember what had happened, she needed every advantage she could get. She'd come to Las Vegas to keep Colin Spencer from marrying Maggie Kelley. And she'd managed that quite nicely by marrying him herself. But if consummation was the only thing standing between them and a quick annulment, then a little white lie was her only recourse.

She needed time—rather, Luke and Maggie needed time. If they really loved each other, they would discover those feelings before too long. And all Isabelle had to do was keep Colin occupied until those feelings took root. There had to be a way to keep him out of Chicago, at least for a few more days.

Isabelle took another sip of coffee and contemplated the man she'd shared a bed with. There was no denying she felt a powerful attraction to him, but she wrote that off as purely physical. Colin Spencer was a handsome man. By all outward appearances, exactly the kind of man she could fall madly in love with.

But lurking beneath the handsome exterior was a stuffy, overbearing, self-absorbed jerk. Sure, there were times when his sexual appeal was almost too much to resist, when just looking at him made her heart race and her blood warm. Isabelle took another gulp of coffee, then slowly set her cup down. "I am not going to let myself fall in love with Colin Spencer," she murmured.

Beyond the physical, he was everything she detested in a man. He was entirely too domineering. He was impatient and pretentious. And he had way too much money—exactly the kind of man her mother wanted her to marry.

"But I have married him," she said, her gaze still fixed on the figure that stood behind the glass wall.

He bent over the sink, leaning closer to the mirror, and she knew he was shaving. Isabelle liked the rough stubble of beard he'd sported earlier that morning. It made him seem a little less polished...more human. But maybe it was better he went back to being the Colin she loved to hate. At least she wouldn't be risking her heart on a man who was still determined to marry her best friend.

He couldn't truly love Maggie, could he? After their conversation in the elevator, she'd concluded his feelings stopped way short of eternal devotion and endless love. So why was he so determined to get back to Chicago? Did he believe there might be something left to salvage?

Isabelle snatched a croissant from a basket of pastries and ripped it apart, stuffing a chunk in her mouth. What if she was wrong? What if Maggie didn't love Luke and Luke didn't love Maggie? And what if Colin loved Maggie instead? If it didn't work out as she'd planned, then she'd lost three friends in one fell swoop. Isabelle frowned. All right, two friends, since she couldn't count Colin as anything more than an acquaintance…and a husband for as long as they managed to remain married.

When he emerged from the bathroom, his hair was still damp and standing up in short spikes. He glanced over at her once, then began to search the room for his clothes. Her gaze fixed on his backside, the damp towel clinging to his bare skin, muscle flexing with every movement as he rummaged through the empty dresser.

He turned and glanced over his shoulder, catching her staring. "Where are my clothes?"

"They're in the closet on the other side of the Jacuzzi," Isabelle offered, a warm flush heating her cheeks.

"Thank you," he said, his voice curt. When he'd gathered up his tux and shoes, he crossed the room to the table. "I've thought about this and there's only one solution to this mess we've gotten into. We need to get a divorce."

Isabelle tossed the remainder of her croissant into the basket, brushed the crumbs from her robe and slowly stood. She braced her palms on the table and leaned toward him, letting her robe gape just a bit. "I don't want a divorce."

His gaze remained firmly on her face. "I don't care what you want. *I* don't want to be married to *you*."

"You should have thought of that before you dragged me in front of a justice of the peace and all those witnesses."

He tossed his clothes aside and slapped his palms on the table, meeting her halfway. His eyes were bright with anger, but he'd controlled his temper to just a tiny twitch in his jaw. "This is not up for debate. If you fight me on this, I'll drag you into court and prove I was not of sound mind and body when I married you."

"Oh, that will be interesting. Colin Spencer admitting he lost control. Stop the presses—this is a big story. And while you're telling the judge you were out of your mind, I'll just have to testify your body was perfectly sound when we crawled into bed together."

The twitch quickened and Isabelle knew she was pushing him too far. If she wasn't careful, he'd walk right out and return to Chicago, spoiling everything she'd worked so hard to accomplish. She drew a deep breath, then stepped back. "All right," she conceded. "What do you want to do?"

"We can't go back to Chicago until we take care of this. I don't want Maggie or my parents finding out about our marriage. We'll get a quickie divorce here and then we can forget this ever happened. I'll call the front desk and ask for the name of an attorney."

He snatched up the phone and punched in a few numbers, while Isabelle continued with her breakfast and her lazy perusal of his body. Though she couldn't tell much from one side of the conversation, she knew Colin wasn't hearing what he wanted to hear. The muscles across his broad shoulders had grown stiff. He finished the call by slamming the phone back down into the cradle. "This is just great," he muttered.

"Good news?"

"We can't get a divorce in Nevada unless we set up residency. We'd have to stay for six weeks. But there are a few places in the phone book that advertise a divorce in ten days."

"Ten days? That's not bad."

Colin cursed, then shook his head. "I can't stay here for ten days! Besides the fact that we can't afford it, I can't be away from work that long."

"Then we'll just have to go back home and take care of this," Isabelle said.

"We are not going home! There has to be another way, someplace where we can get a quick and painless divorce."

Isabelle laughed. "Don't look at me. I've never had occasion to get a divorce." She shook her head. "Call your attorney. I'm sure he'd be able to advise you."

"No!" Colin said. "You and I are the only people in the world who are going to know about this marriage. I'm not going to risk telling anyone, not even my attorney, about this disaster. We'll have to figure this out on our own."

Isabelle sighed, then sat back down in her chair. She poured a fresh cup of coffee then held it out to him. "Mexico," she said.

Colin took a seat next to her, the towel parting to reveal the long length of his leg and hip. "Mexico?"

She drew her eyes away and nodded. "I think you can get an overnight divorce in Tijuana. At least, that's what I've heard."

He let out a tightly held breath and relief flooded his expression. There was no question he was much more handsome when he wasn't so tense. His mouth relaxed and his eyes softened. He almost looked approachable. "We'll go to Tijuana then. We're not far from Mexico."

Isabelle shrugged. "All right, if that's what you want."

"I'll just call the pilot and have him file a flight

plan." He gave her a sheepish look. "Do you remember where we left the plane?"

"You sent the pilot home with the plane. He's back in Chicago."

"Then we'll have to fly commercial."

"Not unless you've got another credit card hidden in that wallet. You don't have enough money for two plane tickets. Unless, of course, you want to call home and ask Daddy to send you a few thousand."

Colin cursed. "How the hell are we supposed to get to Mexico?"

For a guy who was supposed to be so smart, Colin Spencer possessed very little common sense. "We'll have to drive. We can probably rent a car with my credit card. I'm a few hundred short of my limit. And you won enough cash last night that we'll have enough for food and gas. But we'll have to pay for the divorce. That won't come cheap."

He stood up and began to pace in front of her. The towel parted again and again with every step and Isabelle forced her gaze back to her coffee cup. "I can't call home for money," he said. "They'll find out where I am."

"Don't you think the pilot will tell?"

He spun around and stared at her, his hands braced on his narrow waist. "You're right. We can't stay here. What are we going to do? We don't have any money."

Isabelle shook her head in disgust. He had absolutely no imagination at all. He might just as well have been living in a bubble his entire life. Didn't he know how the real world worked? "Where's your watch?" she asked.

"What? Are you late for an appointment?"

"Where's your watch? That big gold thing you were wearing last night."

Colin bent over and picked up his tux trousers, then searched the pockets. He glanced at the watch, then tossed it onto the table. "It's eleven forty-five. Happy?"

Isabelle picked up the Rolex and examined it carefully. "We'll hock it. If it's worth what I think it is, it will give us enough for the divorce."

"Hock it?"

"Sell it at a pawnshop. Or we can try to sell it on the street."

"A pawnshop," he repeated.

"Yes, a pawnshop. Where were you brought up, Pluto? You take this to the pawnshop and the man gives you money and a claim check. If you want your watch back, you buy it back later. If not, the guy sells it. It's very simple. And this town is loaded with pawnshops."

He handed her the watch. "All right, we'll sell the watch."

She examined the timepiece carefully. "How much is it worth?"

Colin shrugged. "I paid five thousand for it."

Isabelle gasped, peering at the watch more closely. "You paid five thousand dollars for a watch and you were upset about losing forty thousand in the casino?"

"I thought you said I lost thirty thousand," he said.

"Thirty, forty, what difference does it make to a guy who wears five thousand on his wrist!" Isabelle hurried over to the table on her side of the round bed and snatched up her own watch. "See this? I paid about seventy dollars for it." She handed his own watch to him. "What time is it?"

"Eleven forty-six," he said.

She handed him her watch. "What time?"

"Eleven forty-six."

Isabelle smiled. "The time comes pretty cheap. And sometimes you can even get it for free if there's a clock in the room."

"That's not the point," he said.

"I understand the point. You wear an expensive watch because you can, not because you need to. I find that awfully pretentious."

"Well, Miss Smarty-Pants, if I didn't own an expensive watch we wouldn't have anything to hock, would we? And if we didn't have anything to hock, we'd both be stuck in this insufferable marriage until death did us part. And the way I feel right now, that wouldn't have been due to natural causes. So, I don't give a damn what you think of me or my Rolex."

He stood up and gathered his clothes, then strode toward the bathroom. "Finish your breakfast and get dressed," he ordered. "We've got to go rent ourselves a car."

Isabelle snatched a muffin from the pastry basket and hurled it at him. It struck him on the back of the head and he stopped. His shoulders tensed, the muscles across his broad back rippling, and she felt sure he'd turn on her. But then, he shook his head and continued to the bathroom. She cursed softly and wrapped her robe more tightly around her body. She'd been married to him for less than seven hours and already he was starting to get on her nerves.

"I guess the honeymoon is just about over," she murmured.

"FIVE HUNDRED DOLLARS," Isabelle cried. "I never thought he'd give us that much for your watch."

Colin watched as Isabelle tucked the money into her purse. He glanced back at the pawnshop, then at Isabelle. No doubt Isabelle's pretty face and the revealing neckline of her gown had helped raise the asking price on his Rolex. The guy in the pawnshop had spent most of the negotiations with his eyes fixed on her cleavage. And to make things worse, Isabelle didn't blink twice before leaning over the counter and giving him a better view. She truly was shameless.

Hell, if Colin had offered to pawn Isabelle herself, he may have gotten twice as much cash. "Don't you feel just a little conspicuous in that dress?" Colin stared down at Isabelle's gown, lingering for only a moment on the daring neckline. After breakfast, they'd slipped into the only clothes they'd brought along, evening wear left over from the night before. Had he known he was going to run away to Las Vegas with Isabelle Channing, he might have packed a change of clothing. And had he known he was going to end up married to her, he might have chosen to jump out of the company jet somewhere over Kansas.

"What's wrong with my dress?" she asked. "Look around you, sport. We're not the only people in bugle beads and black tie. I just saw a lady walking down the street in her wedding gown. Besides, my dress served its purpose in the pawnshop. He was only going to give us three hundred."

Though the revealing cut of her gown might have been appropriate for an evening party, in broad daylight all it elicited was ogling and drooling from the male members of Las Vegas's tourist population. And the enticing view of her breasts wasn't doing him any good either. It wasn't just cleavage, Colin mused. He could have handled that. But whenever she moved, the neckline of her gown shifted and gaped and for a moment Colin could see the perfect curves of her breasts, the exact spot where his hands would come to rest as he slid his palms up to her—

"We've got other business to attend to," he muttered. "And we can't do it dressed like refugees from New Year's Eve."

Colin cursed silently. Was it really the tourists he was worried about? Or was he more concerned about his own endless fascination with her body? Try as he might, he couldn't forget the image of her wrapped in the hotel bathrobe, her body completely naked beneath the plush fabric.

Had he been susceptible to temptation, he might have tossed caution aside and satisfied his curiosity. Was her skin really as smooth as it looked? Would it warm beneath his touch? Would her nipples harden if he brushed his thumbs across them? If he could only remember their wedding night...

Colin sucked in a sharp breath. Something would have to be done about this situation before he completely lost his mind. "We need some new clothes," he said. "The guy at the hotel desk said there's a shopping mall down on the strip."

"We don't have any extra money," Isabelle said.

Colin shot her a sideways glance. "You plan to wear that dress all the way to Mexico?"

"Are you worried about my comfort or are you worried about what people will say? I'm fine in this dress. You're the one with the problem."

He already knew the signs, the narrowed eyes, the slight upward tilt to her chin, the stubborn set of her mouth. Isabelle was itching to go another round, but he didn't have the energy or the inclination to fight with her, not when all he wanted to do was kiss her. "You could walk down the street naked for all I care," he lied. "But I'm wearing a tux that smells of smoke and stale champagne. I want a change of clothes."

"It's not in the budget," she insisted.

"We have the money from the Rolex. We can certainly spare enough for a few items."

"That's for the divorce. And the two hundred in cash is for gas and food. And we can use the last couple hundred on my Visa for the rental car. You're the guy who wanted the quickie divorce. We could always stay here in Vegas and get a divorce in ten days."

"We don't have the cash to stay here for ten days," Colin reminded her.

"You could always take our stake and give gambling another whirl."

"Very funny," Colin murmured.

"And ridiculous. That's why we have to economize. We have just enough to get to Tijuana and arrange an overnight divorce. And nothing more."

Colin held out his hand, fed up with her stingy manner. "Give me fifty dollars. I'll just buy a T-shirt and a pair of jeans."

Isabelle shook her head.

"If memory serves, the money from the Rolex and the gambling winnings are mine. Now give me my money." He reached for her purse, but she yanked it away.

"No!"

Colin ground his teeth. "You can take the fifty dollars out of my share of the food money. I won't eat."

"Oh, please," Isabelle said. "You'd rather be well dressed than well fed?"

"Just give me the damn money, Isabelle! I don't want to have to wrestle you for it."

Thankfully, the look in his eyes was obviously enough to change her mind. If push came to shove, he might have wrestled her, though he was certain his attention would be quickly diverted from the money to the feel of her body beneath his. She gave him a long look, then pulled open her purse and slapped the wad of cash from the Rolex into his outstretched palm. "I'm keeping the two hundred from the gambling. You have the divorce money," she said. "If you spend it all, we're going to have to stay married."

"Believe me, I won't spend it all." He turned, then continued down the street, searching for an available taxi, his arm outstretched. When she didn't follow, he glanced over his shoulder. "Aren't you coming?"

"There's a car-rental place a block over," she said. "Wait here and I'll go get a car. There's no use wasting money on a taxi."

He sat down on a bench and stretched his legs out in front of him. "Get a car with air-conditioning," he called. "A Mercedes or a BMW, if you can."

Isabelle shook her head. "Oh, right. And I won't forget the leather seats and the CD player, either."

"That would be nice," Colin said, "but not necessary."

With a sigh of frustration, she hurried back down the sidewalk to stand in front of him. "Do you live on the same planet as I do or are you some alien from a very wealthy universe? You can't rent a Mercedes for a measly two hundred dollars. I'll rent something cheap."

"Well, make sure it's something cheap with air-conditioning. We have to drive through the desert and it might get hot."

"And I certainly wouldn't want you to get your new clothes all sweaty!" With that, Isabelle turned around and started back down the street. "Be here when I get back," she called. "This exact spot or I'm driving to Chicago and announcing our wedding to the world."

Colin watched her walk away, admiring the provocative sway of her hips as she hurried off. There wasn't anything about Isabelle Channing that didn't tempt and tantalize. The woman was custom made to seduce a man simply by wandering into his field of vision.

"There goes my wife," he murmured. Colin laughed softly. He was probably the envy of any number of men, yet all he wanted was to put Isabelle out of his life for good. He'd made a silly mistake, induced by too much champagne and millennium cheer. But he was determined to correct his error and go on with his life.

He glanced at his watch, then realized he no longer wore a watch. It had to be around one in the afternoon. If he called Luke in Chicago, he might be able to make the first step toward salvaging his engagement to Maggie. Luke was his best friend and Maggie's trusted childhood confidant. If he could get Luke on his side, maybe Luke could exert his influence on Maggie.

As he searched the area for a pay phone, he formulated his strategy. He'd tell Luke he had a few problems to iron out before he came back. "A few problems," he murmured. "One big problem and her name is Isabelle."

He'd ask Luke to watch out for Maggie, to make sure she was taken care of until his return. He wouldn't provide any details—in fact, he wouldn't even mention Isabelle's name. For all he knew, no one was aware they were together. That might be his saving grace. He could write off this whole mess as just a minor case of cold feet.

Now, if he could only make sure his other body parts remained cold. Colin knew that would be a lot easier said than done. Isabelle Channing had an annoying knack for making his blood run hot and his defenses crumble.

4

ISABELLE SAT in the parking lot of the Fashion Show Mall, her fingers rapping impatiently on the steering wheel as she waited for Colin. She'd been sitting in the car for nearly an hour, and this after he'd promised to be in and out in fifteen minutes. If Colin Spencer was anything, he was obsessively prompt. Then again, he no longer owned a watch, so all bets were off.

She loosened her grip on the steering wheel, and hammered on the dashboard with her fist until the radio sputtered back on. Colin had not been pleased when he got a look at the car she'd rented. It was nearly impossible to find transportation in a town filled with millennium revelers. She'd heard the same story at nearly every rental agency she visited. Either their computers were down because of the millennium bug or they were completely out of rental cars she could afford. To make things worse, the bug had struck the air traffic control system and flights were being canceled sporadically all day long. Those who needed to get out of Vegas were forced to leave by car or bus.

If she had wanted to rent a Corvette or a Rolls-Royce, she could have had her pick. But she'd found the ten-year-old Toyota at Acme Auto Rentals and had snapped it up before another tourist desperate to get on the road grabbed it out from under her.

It wasn't such a bad car. The wheels went around when she put it in gear and the horn worked. However, the muffler was about to go south, black exhaust belched out of the tailpipe every time she accelerated and the front end had a shimmy a stripper would envy. She'd rented the car for a hundred and twenty-five for the week with unlimited mileage. That meant they had an extra seventy-five dollars to spend on her credit card, give or take a few dollars. With money like that, she could pick up a simple sundress and a pair of shoes at a discount store on their way out of town.

In truth, she wanted to get out of her "wedding" gown just as much as Colin wanted her to. Her mind drifted back to the ceremony beneath the canopy of lights on Fremont Street. Oddly enough, the wedding was exactly the type of ceremony she might have chosen for herself. Her mother had always planned for the day when Isabelle would walk down the aisle in yards of silk shantung and Belgian lace, surrounded by her mother's Grosse Pointe friends. Isabelle knew she'd never opt for the traditional. If a girl was going to get married, she ought to at least have fun doing it. And the ceremony set in the midst of hundreds of other brides and grooms was certainly memorable.

"Too bad the groom doesn't remember it," she murmured. Regret slowly seeped through her. Maybe she shouldn't have gone so far as to marry him. But when he'd asked her in front of the casino, she'd been carried away by the spontaneity of it all. From the moment she said "I do," she'd been trying to convince herself she'd married him for all the right reasons—mainly, to keep him from marrying Maggie Kelley.

Yet, the more Isabelle thought about it, the more she realized she'd married Colin for all the *wrong* reasons. He was charming and attractive and, when he got enough champagne in him, he was downright fun. And he'd been the first man brave enough to ask her, so she'd felt compelled to accept. And then there had been thoughts of the wedding night...

Isabelle sighed in frustration. She'd never had much luck with men. It wasn't always their fault, since they couldn't help that they were bums and losers. She had just chosen the wrong men, men she couldn't possibly love. Maybe it was a way to protect herself.

From the time she'd begun dating, she'd used her boyfriends as a weapon against her parents, bringing home one unsuitable delinquent after another. Since then, it had become a habit—a habit she couldn't break. Colin Spencer was just another unlikely choice, especially for a husband. Up until the moment they got stuck in the elevator, they'd hated each other.

But that had changed. Why couldn't she summon up the same level of animosity anymore? Maybe because Colin wasn't the man she thought she knew. He wasn't boring; he was just a bit aloof. And the man she once considered stuffy was simply reserved. In truth, she wanted to like him—and she wanted him to like her.

He was an intriguing man and Isabelle had met very few intriguing men in her life. And for all his wealth and power, he was surprisingly unaffected.

Though he'd spent five thousand dollars on a watch, he didn't blink when the pawnshop only paid him five hundred for it. And though he grumbled about her choice of a car, he didn't demand she take it back and exchange it for something more luxurious. He could act like an ordinary guy when the situation demanded.

Her mind wandered back to the early-morning hours, to the not-so-ordinary man she'd crawled into bed with. Isabelle had had a difficult time keeping to her own side of the bed, sorely tempted by his lean, naked form and the possibility of what might happen when he awoke. But she had pushed carnal thoughts aside and, for a long time, had sat beside him, staring down at his face, trying to unravel the riddle of the man she'd married. She'd drifted off to sleep only to wake up curled into the curve of his body, the sheet the only thing between them. Even now, the memory made her feel safe and secure.

If she ever really got married—to a man who remembered the wedding and didn't have a fiancée waiting in another town—she hoped her husband would be a little like Colin. Strong and confident and direct. At least with a man like Colin, she knew exactly where she stood.

"He detests me," she muttered. "He can't wait to divorce me and get back to Maggie." She groaned and pressed her forehead to the steering wheel. It wouldn't do to turn Colin Spencer into her dream man. He'd come to Vegas with her on a whim, a decision made at a vulnerable moment. They'd married without any thought of the gravity of their actions. And now, they'd be forced to spend the next few days together until they could fix the mess they'd made.

A knock sounded on the passenger-side window and Isabelle jumped in surprise. She turned to find Colin standing beside the car. He was dressed in pressed khakis, an expensive polo shirt and a finely tailored sport jacket. In his hands, he clutched a leather suitcase and three large shopping bags.

Isabelle felt her temper rise. She should never have trusted him with the money! He'd gone and spent it all. With a soft curse, she opened the car door and stepped out. Well, if Colin Spencer wanted a divorce, he'd have to figure out how to pay for it himself. She wasn't going to waste any more of her time and energy working out the details.

"Nice clothes," she said, leaning over the roof.

He slowly walked around the front bumper, bending over to examine a broken headlight. "I can't say the same for your choice of transportation, but we were both on a budget."

Isabelle shook her head. She should have been angry, but she wasn't. In truth, she was secretly happy he'd blown their divorce money. Though she was positive she didn't want to be married to Colin Spencer, she wasn't sure yet whether she wanted to divorce him. "You spent it all, didn't you?"

A satisfied smile curled Colin's lips. "I didn't spend a penny." He strolled around the car and handed her four shopping bags. "There's a Neiman Marcus in the mall."

"You couldn't have found something at Sears?"

"I have a credit card for Neiman Marcus. With a very large credit limit—which I maxed out in less than an hour."

"Then, we still have enough for the divorce?" she asked, brushing aside unbidden disappointment.

"Plenty," Colin said. "And I also got a few things for you." He nodded at the bags. "Take a look. I guessed at your size, but I think I came pretty close."

"You bought me something?" she asked, stunned by his generosity and secretly pleased that he'd thought of her.

"Some dresses and a sweater. I hear it gets cold at night in the desert. I knew you needed shoes, but I wasn't sure of your size. So I bought a pair in every size between seven and nine."

Isabelle slowly pulled the clothes from the bag. Colin had bought three colorful cotton dresses with expensive designer labels and a deep blue cashmere sweater. She found a pair of black slacks and a striped T-shirt and a cute little straw hat in the bottom of the first bag. She glanced up at him.

"For the sun," he explained.

She stared at the wardrobe laid out on the hood of the car, amazed at his kindness and his good fashion sense. He'd picked out exactly what she might have, colorful clothes with impeccable styling and just the right amount of flair.

"Do you like everything?" he asked, a hopeful expression on his face. "If you don't, we can go exchange it."

"No," she replied. "Everything is…perfect. It's exactly what I would have bought."

"You like bright colors," he said. "You always wear colorful clothes."

"I—I do." At that moment, she felt the strangest urge to wrap her arms around his neck and kiss him. She was rarely surprised by men, but Colin had left her speechless. He had shopped for her, taking into account her favorite colors as well as her comfort. The second bag was filled with shoe boxes and the third, with toiletries—makeup and perfume, shampoo. He'd also visited the lingerie department, for she found some pretty underwear and a simple cotton nightgown in the fourth bag.

"I didn't pick those out," he said, peering into the bag. "The saleslady did."

"So I guess we're all set."

He nodded. "I guess we are." Colin stepped back and took another long look at the car. "Too bad they don't have rental cars at Neiman Marcus." He shook his head. "I tried to get them to give me a cash advance on the store card, but they wouldn't, so I bought this." He held out his wrist.

"You bought a new watch?"

"If we run out of money, we can hock this one," he said. "I guess it's kind of like a cash advance." He reached into his pocket and withdrew a small jewelry box, then handed it to her. "Open it."

Holding her breath, Isabelle flipped open the lid. Inside she found a simple diamond ring of at least a carat or two, so perfect that she couldn't imagine a ring she'd like better. She swallowed hard as she examined it, the round stone winking in the bright sunlight. "I—I don't understand."

"Something else to hock," he said with a shrug. "Just in case. Go ahead, put it on."

"I—I don't think that—"

He took the box from her hand, grabbed the ring and pushed it onto her finger. "You won't lose it this way."

Isabelle drew a ragged breath, then nodded. "Good thinking."

They stared at each other for a long moment, her gaze captured by his. A slow shiver skittered up her spine and she almost pushed up onto her toes to kiss him. At the least, she felt the need to say something, to tell him how thoughtful he was, to apologize for the nasty way she'd treated him, for all the disparaging things she'd said about him and his money. But in a single instant, she knew the feelings welling up inside her were wrong. She couldn't possibly allow herself to fall in love with Colin Spencer, not even just a little bit. Not even for just a little while.

"We should go," she finally said.

"Give me the keys. I'll drive."

Isabelle blinked, startled by his suddenly autocratic demand. She slowly put all his purchases back in the bags as her temper simmered. This was exactly why she couldn't possibly fall in love with Colin Spencer. He was overbearing and arrogant! "No, you won't drive," she said. "I rented the car, I'll drive. Besides, I wouldn't trust you behind the wheel."

"And why not?"

She gave him a condescending look. "Don't you let your chauffeur do most of your driving, Mr. Moneybags?" Her comment cut to the quick and she instantly regretted provoking him. Why was there no middle ground between lust and lashing him with her tongue?

"I can drive the damn car, Isabelle. You can navigate. Now give me the keys."

With a vivid curse, she tossed the keys at his face, more angry with herself than with him. There were times when being with Colin seemed to bring out the best in her. There were other moments when he turned her into a sharp-tongued harpy.

The moment before the keys hit his nose, he reached up and caught them. A satisfied smirk played across his lips. "Thank you," he said.

"This divorce couldn't come soon enough," she muttered, hoisting up her shopping bags.

"I hope you put gas in the car because we're not stopping until we get to Mexico."

As she walked around to the other side of the car, Isabelle couldn't help but glance down at the diamond ring on her finger. He could have bought earrings or a necklace just as easily. Or another watch. Why had he chosen a diamond ring?

She yanked open the back door of the car and tossed the bags inside. Trying to figure out Colin Spencer's motives was a waste of time. He'd married her after too much champagne and, now sober, he wanted a divorce. He had no ulterior motives. The clothes he'd purchased for her were not a gift, but an underhanded way of telling her he didn't care for her dress. And the diamond was simply money in the bank, not some secret sign of his unspoken devotion.

She slammed the door, then drew a deep breath. Everything was moving so quickly and there didn't seem to be any way to slow it down. Though she hadn't given her marriage to Colin Spencer more than a moment's thought, her divorce from him was a different matter. Now that they were husband and wife, their marriage vows had taken on a whole new meaning.

"The former Mrs. Colin Spencer," she murmured under her breath, staring out the window as the car pulled away from the curb. "I'm not sure I like the sound of that."

"Do you have to change in the car? I can just as easily pull over at a gas station."

Colin glanced over at Isabelle in time to see her tugging one of her new dresses over her head. Though he'd bought her a bra to go with the panties, she'd chosen not to put it on and he was treated to a fleeting glimpse of her breasts.

What was this odd fascination with Isabelle's body? She had the same basic parts as every other woman on the planet. But it was the way those parts fit together that intrigued and tempted him. Every time he looked at her, he found it harder to ignore the odd attraction sparking between them, the uneasy desire for a woman he should, by all accounts, hate.

"You're the one who wanted to get to Mexico so fast." She glanced over at him as she shimmied out of her gown, reaching up under the sundress and pulling the gown down to her feet. "And keep your eyes on the road."

"You're the navigator," he said, embarrassed to be caught gawking. "Shouldn't you be watching the road?"

"Just stay on Highway 93. It will take us right to the Hoover Dam."

"The Hoover Dam? We're driving to the Hoover Dam?"

"Yeah, the Hoover Dam," she said, tossing her gown into the back seat. She twisted around and began to rummage through the boxes of shoes until she found a pair that fit. "I've always wanted to see it. And we've only gone a few miles out of the way."

"This isn't on the way to Mexico?" Colin asked. He already knew the answer to his question. He also knew he never should have trusted Isabelle with the map. He should have carefully studied the route, memorized the directions and confiscated the map before he put the car into gear.

"It will be very educational. The Hoover Dam is a modern engineering marvel."

Colin cursed. This was just like Isabelle, flying off on some ridiculous tangent. "I don't care what it is! We're in the middle of bumper-to-bumper traffic on a narrow, winding highway through the mountains in a car that hasn't had a brake job in ten years and you're telling me we're not even on our way to Mexico?"

She gave him an innocent look. "Did you know the top of the Hoover Dam is 726 feet above the riverbed?"

"You've studied the Hoover Dam?"

"No, I read it on a sign a few miles back."

Colin reached across the seat, grabbed the map and arranged it in front of him on the steering wheel. "I knew I shouldn't have let you navigate," he grumbled. "What's next? Mount Rushmore? With your rather questionable map-reading skills, I'm sure that's on the way to Mexico, too."

Isabelle sighed and slouched in the seat. "Do you have to be such a wet blanket? This could be very interesting. And there are probably bathrooms, which I am in serious need of right now. Maybe we can buy something cold to drink, maybe even get something to eat."

Colin crumpled the map and shoved it down around her feet. "Isabelle, we've been in the car for less than an hour. If we keep going at this rate, we'll get to Mexico next Christmas."

She snatched up the map and methodically refolded it. "There's no reason why we can't make this trip pleasant—and educational. It doesn't all have to be about divorce, does it?"

He drew a long breath, then let it out slowly. "That's what it *is* about. Divorce. That's precisely why we're going to Mexico. Because you and I made a huge mistake and now we have to fix it."

"Fine," she murmured. "We'll fix it right after we see the Hoover Dam. Just keep driving because this highway takes us right over the top. After we get a look, we can turn around and go get your stupid divorce." She wriggled over to the far side of the seat, crossing her arms over her chest and fixing her gaze on the landscape passing by the window.

Silence, tempered with anger, filled the cramped interior of the Toyota. It was impossible to dislike Isabelle, Colin mused. The more time he spent with her, the more he was beginning to appreciate her unique personality and enthusiastic outlook on life. And she certainly wasn't hard to look at, especially when she was offering up such enticing views of her body.

Under the right circumstances, he might find her completely captivating. But he had a fiancée waiting for him back in Chicago. And a family who would never welcome a woman like Isabelle Channing with open arms. She had to know how desperate his situation was, how important it was they got their divorce and went home as quickly as possible.

He glanced her way and a reluctant smile touched his lips. She really was a stunning woman. In the low light of a Las Vegas night, she had looked exotic and alluring. But by day, Isabelle possessed a fresh-faced beauty, with her ivory skin and nearly black hair. He watched as she tucked an errant strand of hair behind her ear. The diamond ring glinted in the light and Colin was hit with the sudden realization he was a married man.

Less than twenty-four hours ago, he'd been preparing to announce his engagement to Maggie Kelley. He'd been ready to settle down and build a life with her. Everything had been so neatly planned—until he'd taken that first sip of champagne.

Could he really blame all this on champagne? Nothing could have made him walk out on Maggie if he had truly loved her. Maybe he was looking for an excuse to escape and he found it in the elevator with Isabelle. She'd merely opened his eyes and made him look at the rest of his life in an honest way. And he hadn't liked what he'd seen.

Maggie Kelley was a wonderful woman. But there was no fire, not even a spark between them. For once, he had wanted to live life dangerously, to see what it was like to push the edges of propriety. He just hadn't expected to tumble right over that edge into a marriage with Isabelle Channing.

At least there were sparks. Hell, he and Isabelle Channing were like matches and gasoline, an explosion just waiting to happen. Or waiting to happen again, according to Isabelle. Colin frowned. How could he possibly have forgotten making love to her? He remembered bits and pieces of the rest of the evening. Even the wedding. And he vaguely recalled returning to the hotel room and slipping out of his jacket. After that, everything was a big blank.

Staring out at the traffic ahead of him, he tried to summon up just a shred of their time together in bed. But every image that drifted into his mind had no basis in reality. Though he'd never touched her hair, he sensed how it would feel, running between his fingers like warm silk. Her mouth would taste like honey and her skin would smell like roses. And when he put his hands on her perfect breasts, soft, urgent sounds would slip from her throat.

A knot of desire tightened in his belly and he drew in a ragged breath. It had probably been quite passionate, considering the level of desire mere thought brought forth. Isabelle was not a woman who brought inhibition into the bedroom. With a woman like her, a man could lose himself in pure, unadulterated lust. Every other woman he'd ever had would pale compared to Isabelle.

"So why can't I remember?" he murmured.

"What?"

Colin blinked, then turned to find Isabelle watching him, her eyes wide with curiosity. "Nothing," he said. "Just thinking out loud."

A few minutes later the road opened up and the dam came into view. Jagged rocks thrust from the canyon walls, rising up on either side of the Colorado River, the river cutting deeply into the earth. On one side, a huge lake shimmered in the sun, the water glistening around a string of towers that extended from the dam. On the other side there was nothing but empty space, dropping hundreds of feet to the river.

Colin had to admit the sight was breathtaking, the sheer magnitude of the dam was mind-boggling.

And to think he'd nearly missed seeing it, had it not been for Isabelle.

"Look at all those people," she said, pointing out the window. "What are they wearing on their heads?"

Colin stared at the tourists lining the walkways on both sides of the dam. "I don't know. They all have on the same hat. You can probably buy one in the gift shop if you like it that much."

"It's not a hat." Isabelle frowned. "It looks like a little pyramid covered with tinfoil. Why would they all be wearing tinfoil on their heads?"

The answer came soon enough. As they slowly approached the dam, Colin noticed a banner hanging from a railing. "Welcome Extraterrestrials," he read. "I think these people are aliens."

"They're not aliens," Isabelle said. "They're waiting for aliens!" She giggled and clapped her hands. "Oh, this is exciting. I've been reading about this. There are a lot of people who think aliens will invade Earth on the millennium. And we just happened upon the very spot they're going to land!"

Colin shot her a dubious look. "I should have guessed you and these loony tunes had something in common. You believe in space aliens?"

She glanced over at him and rolled her eyes. "Were you born a curmudgeon or was that a talent you developed over time?"

"I am not a curmudgeon."

"Anyone named after a part of the human digestive system is destined to be a little constipated in the head."

"My name is Colin, not colon."

"It's hard to tell the difference sometimes," Isabelle said, her voice filled with sarcasm.

With a soft curse, Colin pulled the car into the parking lot. His patience was almost at an end when he finally found a parking space and swung the Toyota into it. He shut off the ignition and turned to Isabelle. "If we expect to get through the next few days without killing each other, we'd better call a truce right now."

Isabelle gave him a lethal look, then jumped out of the car. For a moment, Colin wasn't going to follow her. She could jump over the edge of the dam for all he cared. Then he realized he didn't exactly trust all these crazies with tinfoil pyramids on their heads. He shoved the door open and ran after her, catching up to her in a few long strides.

"Just leave me alone," she said. "I'm going to look at the damn dam."

He grabbed her hand, but she yanked out of his grasp and continued on her way. Colin cursed again. "You've been impossible since we left Vegas," he said. "How long are you going to pout about not driving?"

"That's not why I hate you," she yelled.

"Well, tell me what I did to deserve your wrath. Enlighten me, Isabelle, because I don't know what the hell you want from me."

He followed her onto the walkway, skirting the edge of the dam. Isabelle bent over the concrete and stared into the vast expanse of space where a river had once flowed in prehistoric times. Now there was nothing but air and a wide wall of concrete holding back millions of gallons of water. Colin felt a surge of vertigo and he wanted to pull her back, to keep her safe.

The cool wind snapped at her dress and Isabelle hugged her arms to her body. "You're shivering," he murmured. Colin slipped out of his sport jacket and draped it over her shoulders, then gently turned her around to face him. She refused to meet his gaze. He tipped her chin up with his fingers, forcing her eyes to his.

For an instant, he thought about kissing her, about leaning forward ever so slightly and brushing his lips against hers. But he pushed aside the urge, determined not to be drawn in by her pretty face and pouty lips. "What do you want from me?"

"Nothing," she replied, clutching the lapels of his jacket.

"Isabelle, we've got a long trip in front of us. The way I figure, we're going to be driving over four hundred miles together. We can't go on like this. I want to make peace."

She leaned back against the railing and bit at her bottom lip. "You just make me so angry sometimes."

"Why? Because of the clothes? Or was it the crack I made about the aliens?" Frustration flooded her expression, color rising in her cheeks. She looked so pretty when she was angry…and when she was calm…and when she was excited.

"No!" Isabelle cried. "It's because you're so anxious to divorce me! You can hardly wait to get to Mexico. Is marriage to me that abhorrent?"

Colin's jaw dropped. He'd expected a logical answer. Instead, he got the female mind at work, convoluted reasoning and baffling conclusions. "That's what you're upset about?"

"What woman wouldn't be?" she asked. "I know we didn't get married under the best of circumstances. I know you had too much to drink. But you still asked me to marry you and I accepted. I'm your wife and you could treat me just a little nicer."

Colin drew a deep breath and made a valiant attempt to see things through her eyes. He hadn't been very nice. But he also had assumed Isabelle harbored no feelings of affection for him at all. She'd married him in a moment of sheer spontaneity, a decision he thought she regretted as much as he did. He sighed and raked his hands through his hair. "I'm sorry. You're right. I've been rude and obnoxious."

"You should be sorry," she said with a sniff.

He wasn't sure what insanity possessed him at that exact moment, whether it was the vulnerable look in her eyes, or whether it was the notion Isabelle might care about him just a little bit. Or maybe it was all the tempting fantasies he'd had since he crawled out of bed that morning. But it seemed like the most natural thing in the world to lean over and kiss her cheek. And it would have been completely innocent had he stopped there.

As Colin slowly pulled back, temptation drew his gaze to her sweet mouth. Slowly, he brought his lips down on hers, intending to linger for a fleeting moment. The kiss was gentle at first and he felt her hesitate. But she didn't make a move to stop him and he couldn't stop himself. He traced the crease in her lips with his tongue until she opened her mouth to him.

The taste of her set his senses reeling and Colin slipped his hands around her waist and pulled her against his body. All the people around them dissolved into the distance as every thought focused on the touch of her lips, the feel of her body beneath his hands. His palms slid up her rib cage until he could feel the soft flesh of her breasts beneath his fingers.

She moaned softly and the sound brought him back to reality. Reluctantly, Colin drew his hands away. His mouth hovered over hers for a long moment and instinct told him to kiss her again. But they were in the middle of a crowd of tinfoil-topped tourists. And if he kissed her again, he'd be tempted to do things that weren't fit for public viewing, even by people open-minded enough to believe in aliens.

Isabelle cleared her throat, then looked up at him with an uneasy smile. "Incredible," she murmured.

"Yeah," he replied, sneaking another quick kiss. "It was pretty amazing."

She blushed and turned away. "I—I mean, the dam."

"Oh, right," he said, quickly covering his mistake with a shrug. "The dam."

He didn't give a damn about the dam! Had they been any other place but at one of the wonders of American engineering, he would have found some quiet spot and continued his intimate study of her mouth. But there was nowhere to go, no place to steal just one more kiss.

"I'm cold," she said. "I'm going to go back to the car and get my sweater. Can I have the keys?"

Colin reached into his pants' pocket and held them out to her. "Do we have a truce?" he asked softly.

She handed him his jacket. "I'm not going to steal the car and drive off without you, if that's what you're afraid of," she said.

"That's not what I'm asking."

Isabelle sighed. "All right. We have a truce. At

least until the next time you say something boorish or condescending."

He grinned. "I'll try to hold my tongue."

"I'll meet you back here in a few minutes." She turned and walked toward the parking lot. Colin watched her until she disappeared into the crowd. He thought he understood Isabelle Channing, but he suddenly realized there was much more beneath the surface. She'd always seemed so tough, so resilient, as if no man could touch her heart. But a few misplaced words was all it had taken to crack that fragile facade.

He'd hurt her. He'd married her and then, without a single ounce of remorse, had decided to toss the marriage aside. Even a woman with ice water running through her veins would feel some trace of rejection. And Colin knew Isabelle's heart was not as cold as she'd made it out to be.

He would have to be more understanding, more accepting. And when it came time to end their short marriage, he'd have to come to grips with the fact that Isabelle might have her own regrets.

What he didn't want to acknowledge was that she might also be experiencing some of the same attraction he'd tried so hard to ignore. If he fell in love with Isabelle Channing, he knew he could put his feelings aside and get back to life as he knew it. But if Isabelle fell in love with him, Colin was certain disaster wasn't too far behind.

He'd just have to make sure she didn't fall in love with him.

ISABELLE SAT in the stall, her elbows braced on her knees, her chin cupped in her hand. She'd been hid-ing in the bathroom for nearly fifteen minutes, trying to sort out what was going on between her and Colin Spencer.

He had kissed her! Right out of the blue and for no apparent reason, he'd leaned over and covered her mouth with his. The electricity generated by the Hoover Dam paled in comparison to what she felt when his lips touched hers. Isabelle brought her fingers to her mouth and sighed softly.

This man had the power to make her blood sing and her heart pound. This man who drove her crazy, who pricked her temper and tested her resolve at every turn. She didn't want to fall in love with him, but that was impossible when he kept her as off balance as he had. One moment, she hated him and the next, she wanted to fall into his arms and give herself over to his touch.

Maybe she shouldn't have agreed to the truce. It was much easier to hate Colin Spencer when he was acting like a jerk. She mentally calculated how long it would take to drive the four hundred miles to Tijuana. At fifty miles an hour, it should take eight hours. Just eight hours more, alone in a car, with Colin Spencer.

But it was already past three in the afternoon. Even if they left now, they'd probably be forced to stop for the night somewhere along the way—in a motel, with just enough money for one room. Isabelle swallowed hard, then slipped on the cashmere cardigan he'd bought her. They'd just have to drive straight through.

She sighed as the soft sweater warmed her arms. Isabelle bought most of her clothes at vintage boutiques and secondhand shops. Her budget didn't allow for expensive designer clothes. But she had to admit the dress was worth every penny. It fit perfectly, hugging her torso and flaring out into a skirt that ended just above the ankle. And it made her feel pretty and confident and a little proper, the kind of woman Colin Spencer might find attractive.

"Stop it!" she scolded. "What do you care what Colin Spencer thinks?" With a soft curse, she stood up and exited the stall. She would put these silly feelings aside and remind herself every few minutes that Colin Spencer was exactly the kind of man her mother wanted her to marry. That should be enough reason to keep him at a distance.

As Isabelle walked back to where she'd left Colin, she noticed an elderly woman standing along the road, a sign clutched in her hands and a foil-covered pyramid perched on her head. She wore a pair of plaid capri pants, a Born to Play Bingo T-shirt and battered running shoes. Crude lettering spelled out San Diego on the small piece of cardboard she held and Isabelle knew in an instant she'd found the solution to all her problems.

"A chaperone," she murmured. "That's exactly what I need on this trip."

She strode up to the woman and pointed to her sign. "Are you looking for a ride to San Diego?"

The elderly woman smiled, her face breaking into a road map of deep wrinkles, the little pyramid bouncing around on her white curls. "Would you be going that way?"

Isabelle nodded. "My friend—I mean, my husband and I are taking a little drive down to Tijuana. That's not far from San Diego, is it?"

"Oh, no, dear. You have to go right through San Diego to get to Tijuana."

"What's your name?" Isabelle asked.

"Omega Seven," the old woman said. "But you can call me Edith. I've been waiting for the mother ship, but there seems to have been a mix-up. It was supposed to be here at midnight last night. Midnight on the millennium."

"The mother ship?" Isabelle asked.

"Yes. I've been waiting to get back home after nearly thirty years on this planet."

Isabelle gave her an indulgent smile, nodding as the woman spoke and wondering just how crazy Edith was. "Then you're an alien?"

"I prefer extraterrestrial. Or nonhuman life-form. Though I do inhabit a human body."

"And you live in San Diego?"

She nodded. "I'm retired from the post office. There are lots of us working at government jobs. It's part of the strategy to assimilate. I was only supposed to be here for ten years, but my assignment was too important."

"Sorting the mail?"

Edith leaned closer, her voice lowering to a conspiratorial whisper. "I read it all," she said. "I have X-ray vision and a photographic memory. I know everything about everyone in the whole 92101 area code."

"Well, that's fine," Isabelle said with a smile, patting her on the shoulder. Edith was obviously harmless. A little deluded, but harmless. "I can hardly wait for you to meet my husband. He'll find you very…fascinating."

"Is your husband an extraterrestrial?" Edith asked, picking up her battered carpetbag.

Isabelle grasped Edith's elbow, then headed them both back toward Colin. "I'm not sure what he does, but it involves making a lot of money."

Edith shot her a curious glance. "He's your husband and you don't know what he does for a living?"

"Actually, we've only been married a day," Isabelle explained. "Less than a day."

"Then you're on your honeymoon! Oh, how romantic."

"No," Isabelle said. "The honeymoon was over a few minutes after we got married. We're going to Tijuana to get a divorce."

Edith shook her head. "Oh, this is a sad thing. My husband, Floyd, and I have been married for nearly forty years. Marriage is very difficult, especially a mixed marriage."

"He's not an alien?"

She lowered her voice. "He's Episcopalian, dear. But we worked hard at it. I'm sure if you and your husband talked about your problems, you could save your marriage."

"I don't think so," Isabelle said. "And it would probably be best not to mention it to Colin. We'll be happy to drop you off in San Diego, but then we're going to Tijuana for a divorce. That's already been settled."

Edith sighed. "All right, dear. If you insist. But I still think you're making a mistake."

Colin was waiting for her when she walked up. He watched as she approached, his arms crossed over his broad chest, his body leaning against the railing.

When he noticed Edith at her side, a frown creased his forehead.

"He looks a bit perturbed," Edith said. "Are you sure this is all right?"

"He always looks perturbed," Isabelle explained. When she reached his side, she forced a smile. "Colin Spencer, this is Omega Seven," she said, nodding in Edith's direction. "Omega, this is my *husband*, Colin. Omega and I just met. She's going to San Diego and I said she could ride along with us."

Colin shot Isabelle a look of disbelief, then reached out and took Isabelle's hand. "It's a pleasure to meet you, Miss...Seven, but would you excuse us for a few minutes. I need to talk to my *wife*." The last word was said with just enough undisguised aggravation to indicate a refusal would not be recommended.

"I'll be right back," Isabelle said, giving Edith a pat on the hand.

His fingers bit into her elbow as Colin led her away down the sidewalk. When they'd walked out of earshot, he turned her around to face him. His expression had deteriorated from aggravation to pure anger. "What the hell do you think you're doing? We are not driving that woman to San Diego."

"It's right on the way," Isabelle said. "What's the problem?"

"The problem is, she's a complete stranger. And she's wearing a pyramid on her head. We're not letting some crazy person into our car. Don't you read the papers, Isabelle?"

"Edith wouldn't hurt a fly. She's a perfectly nice old lady. And if you had any compassion at all, you'd let her ride with us. She was standing on the walkway ready to stick out her thumb. She could do a lot worse than us for a ride to San Diego."

"No!" Colin said. "I forbid it."

"You what?"

"I said, I forbid it. I will not allow some stranger in our car."

"You *forbid* it?" Isabelle clenched her fists and ground her teeth, taking a step forward until she was toe-to-toe with Colin. "You have no right to tell me what I can and cannot do."

"I have every right. You're my wife, Isabelle, and it's my responsibility to look after your welfare. We will not let that woman into our car. End of discussion." He turned on his heel and started toward the parking lot.

"If she doesn't go, then I don't go," Isabelle called. "And without me, you can't get your divorce."

He stopped short, then slowly turned back to her. "That's blackmail."

"That's the deal," she said.

His fists clenched at his sides and he muttered a vivid oath. In the end, he accompanied them both to the car, opened the back door and helped Edith inside. When Isabelle approached, he yanked open the driver's door and ushered her behind the wheel. "From now on, I'll do the navigating."

Isabelle smiled to herself as she put the key into the ignition. Maybe all the fighting was worth it. For the first time since they'd left Chicago, she felt as if she had Colin Spencer exactly where she wanted him—right under her thumb.

5

"COLIN?" Isabelle reached across the seat and grabbed his shoulder, giving him a desperate shake. He'd fallen asleep a few miles back, the map spread across his lap, and she hadn't wanted to wake him. They'd been headed south for nearly two hours on a desolate stretch of Highway 95 and so far the trip had been uneventful. But when Edith pulled out the gun, Isabelle figured he ought to know. "Colin, wake up!"

His eyes fluttered once, then opened and, with a yawn, he stretched and sat up in the seat. "What's wrong?"

Isabelle glanced in the rearview mirror, and forced a bright smile. "Nothing's wrong. It's just that Edith wants us to change our itinerary. She wants us to drive her to Roswell."

Colin rubbed his eyes. "Roswell? Is that on the way to Tijuana?" he asked in a sleepy voice.

Isabelle winced. "No. It's in New Mexico. But I really don't think we should refuse."

Colin frowned, then glanced over his shoulder to see what Isabelle had been staring at for the past ten minutes in the rearview mirror. With a trembling hand, Edith aimed the gun at Colin's head. He blinked once, then chuckled. "What is that? One of those alien ray guns?"

"No, it's a real gun," Isabelle said, grabbing his arm and turning him back around. "Just be quiet and let's do as she says."

A sigh of disbelief slipped from his lips and she glanced over at him, her mind jumping back to all the warnings he'd given her about picking up strangers. Why hadn't she listened to him? Why hadn't she trusted his instincts instead of her own? This was all her fault and if they ended up shot dead and lying in a ditch in the desert, she'd never forgive herself.

"I—I'm sorry," she whispered. "I guess I made another error in judgment."

He reached out and placed his hand on her thigh. The instant he touched her, she felt the blood drain from her limbs and go straight to her heart. She didn't want to die. Not here and not now. She wasn't done living her life yet; there were still things she wanted to do. But none of those things came immediately to mind. Instead, Isabelle found herself thinking about Colin, about how she wanted more time with him.

"Don't worry," he murmured, his voice calm and soothing. "I won't let anything happen to you."

Edith leaned forward, a wide smile on her flushed face. "When I join the mother ship, they'll give me my own disrupter," she said. "I could blast you with that and your atoms would be scattered all over this car."

"There'll be no atom scattering here," Colin said in a friendly tone. He dropped his voice to a whisper. "Isabelle, stop the car."

She shook her head. "No. Edith wants us to take her to Roswell. This highway runs into the interstate about twenty miles down the road and that will take us right to New Mexico."

Edith waved her gun around as she spoke. "Everyone thought they'd land at the Hoover Dam. All the hydroelectric generators are like a homing device for our spacecraft. I should have known they'd be coming down in New Mexico. But then, they could be coming down at Area 51. That would be north of Las Vegas." Edith leaned back in the seat to ponder the possibility while Isabelle tried to fend off her own nervous collapse.

"Isabelle, pull over, right now."

Though still barely a whisper, his voice was hard and unyielding and she did as she was told, taking her foot off the accelerator. When the car bumped to a stop on the dusty shoulder of the highway, Colin reached over, took her hand and pressed his lips to her wrist. He looked up at her, urging her to obey with just his eyes. "Edith, we're going to let Isabelle get out now. I'll be driving you to Roswell, all right?"

"I don't care who drives, dear. Just as long as I get there before the mother ship takes off."

Isabelle shook her head, but Colin gave her hand a squeeze. "There'll be another car coming along soon. It's all right. You'll be safe." He reached into his back pocket and took out his wallet. "Take the money and go home. I'll see you back in Chicago."

"I don't want you to go without me," Isabelle pleaded. She couldn't let him put his life in danger to protect hers. Colin was her husband. They'd promised to take care of each other, for better or for worse. Having a crazy old lady pointing a handgun at their heads would definitely qualify as worse. "I'm going to stay with you."

"I'll be fine," Colin insisted. "Edith and I will drive to Roswell. Then I'll come home to Chicago. I promise, I'll see you there. Now, go on. Do as I say."

She felt tears press at the corners of her eyes. This was all her fault! She couldn't just walk away without trying to fix it. "No, I won't," Isabelle said, frustration creeping into her voice. "We go together, or we don't go at all."

"Damn it, Isabelle, for once in your life, would you do as you're told. I'm trying to protect you and you're turning this into another attack on your independence."

"I told you before that you can't order me around and I—"

"Stop it!" Edith cried. She pointed the gun at Isabelle and then at Colin. "Give me that wallet." Frightened, Isabelle tossed it over the seat and Edith took out their divorce money and carefully counted it, before she tucked it into her carpetbag and returned the wallet to Colin. "Now, both of you, get out of the car. I've had just about enough of your bickering."

Isabelle closed her eyes and said a silent prayer. Why hadn't she kept her mouth shut? It wasn't wise to irritate the person with the gun. Reluctantly, Isabelle pushed open the driver's-side door and stepped outside. She watched as Colin stepped out of his side and slowly circled the car until he reached her. With careful steps, they backed away from the car, descending from the edge of the road into the low brush of the surrounding desert. "Do you think she's going to shoot us?" Isabelle asked, clutching at his arm.

He gently maneuvered her behind him, until he

stood squarely between her and the muzzle of Edith's gun. "If she does shoot, I want you to run. She's an old lady. She won't be able to catch you. Run as fast and as far as you can. Do you understand?"

"I'm not—"

The muscles in his broad back tensed beneath her fingers. She didn't have to see his face to know his jaw had gone tight and his eyes had turned hard. His tolerance had reached its limit. "Isabelle, I don't want you to argue. Just say you'll do as I tell you."

She drew in a sharp breath as she peeked around his shoulder and saw Edith stepping out of the back seat. The old woman bent over and pulled Isabelle's shopping bags and Colin's new suitcase from the car, then placed them neatly on the side of the road.

"She wouldn't leave our things if she was planning to shoot us, would she?" Isabelle asked.

"Don't ask me to predict the actions of a certified psycho," he muttered.

"She is not a psycho. She's just desperate to get to the mother ship."

"When they issue your license to practice psychiatry, let me know. I'll move to Greenland."

When Edith had finished taking all their belongings out of the car, she set the gun down on top of Colin's suitcase. With a cheery wave, she slipped behind the wheel of the Toyota and shut the door. "Thank you for the ride," she called. "You earthlings are generous people!" A few seconds later, all that was left of Omega Seven, aka Edith, their rental car and their divorce money was a cloud of dust.

Isabelle slowly emerged from behind Colin and they stood staring off into the distance as the car disappeared over the horizon. For a long time, they didn't speak. She waited patiently for Colin to tear into her, to shout out his "I-told-you-sos" and chastise her for her stupidity. Instead, he simply sighed and took her hand, lacing her fingers through his. "I hope you didn't put a big deposit down on that car."

Isabelle gave him a sideways glance, the irony of his words slowly sinking in. She laughed once, then again, and before long, she couldn't seem to stop laughing. Isabelle clutched onto his arm to steady herself. Hysteria had nearly taken over when Colin dropped her hand and stalked to their bags at the edge of the road.

He picked up the gun, then with a curse, heaved it out into the desert. It came to rest in a clump of sagebrush. "It's plastic," he shouted. "It's a toy. I told you it was a ray gun."

Another wave of laughter overcame Isabelle and she sat down where she stood, burying her face in her hands and trying to stem the tears running down her cheeks. When she'd finally calmed herself, she looked up to find Colin standing over her, his lean body outlined by the late-afternoon sun, his broad shoulders blocking the glare from her eyes.

"This isn't funny," he said.

"Oh, yes, it is. Look at us," Isabelle replied, her voice still trembling with suppressed laughter. "We're both from Chicago. We're street-smart. And we let a little old lady with a plastic gun steal our car. I think that's pretty darn funny."

Colin reached down and grabbed her hands, then pulled Isabelle to her feet. "We'll see how funny it is when we're stuck out here in the middle of the night with the snakes and coyotes."

"Snakes and coyotes would be a snap compared to old Edith and her ray gun," Isabelle said.

"Come on," he muttered. "There's a town about five miles down the road. I noticed a sign just before you pulled off the highway. If we can't catch a ride, we can walk there before the sun goes down."

Isabelle fell into step beside him. They grabbed their things and set off at a brisk pace down the narrow strip of asphalt. In truth, Isabelle was glad to be out of the car. The scenery all around them, though starkly desolate, had a wild and exciting beauty to it. In the distance, on either side of the highway, she could see low mountain ranges. Misshapen trees huddled together in clumps and everything was a rich shade of brown. And though she knew the desert was filled with all sorts of wildlife, she wasn't at all afraid, not with Colin at her side.

"I want to thank you for protecting me," Isabelle said after they'd traipsed a far bit down the road. "No one's ever done something like that for me."

"You mean this is the first time you—and the man you married in a Las Vegas wedding—have been carjacked in the middle of the desert by an old lady with a tinfoil pyramid on her head?"

"No, I'm pretty sure that was the first time," Isabelle said. She paused for a long moment, standing at the edge of the highway. He walked a few steps ahead of her, then stopped. "How come you're not mad at me? I mean, this whole thing is my fault. I wanted to give Edith a ride."

"I was angry, but only until she drove off," he turned around. "Once she was gone, all I could feel was relief. I was just happy nothing had happened to you—I mean, to us."

A slow smile curled Isabelle's lips. She stepped up to his side and slipped her hand into his. "You're not such a bad husband," she said in a teasing voice, "even if you are a little dictatorial."

He looked down at her and a reluctant grin broke across his handsome face. "And you're not such a bad wife, except that you never listen to me."

"Are we going to have another argument?" she asked.

"We called a truce," he said. "Don't you remember?"

Isabelle nodded. "So, what are we going to do for money?"

Colin shrugged. "You've got the two hundred I won at blackjack. And we've got the watch and the ring. And my credit cards, for what they're worth."

"I don't think there's a Bloomingdale's out this way."

"We'll figure everything out once we get to town."

As she walked beside him, Isabelle contemplated all that had happened over the past few hours. And as she reexamined each little event in greater detail, she was forced to admit Colin Spencer made a very good husband. When faced with a crisis, he was cool and composed, his only thought for her safety. Somehow, those qualities suddenly outweighed all the negatives she'd worked so hard to attach to his personality.

Isabelle sighed softly and stole another look at his profile, limned gold by the sinking desert sun. If a girl had to be married, she mused, Colin Spencer wasn't such a bad catch after all.

"WE ARE NOT GOING to steal a car," Colin said. He grabbed Isabelle's arm and dragged her away from the garishly lit gas station and used-car lot in Skull Creek, California. The town was too small to appear on the map. In truth, it was just a motley collection of buildings—a roadhouse, a cheap motel, a grocery store, the gas station and some rundown houses. The sign at the edge of town claimed two hundred inhabitants and Colin suspected they were all visiting the Happy Jackrabbit Saloon.

"It's not that hard," she said, pointing to a row of cars at the rear of the gas station. "All those cars have For Sale signs in the windows. We'll just boost one of them and send the owner the money later. It wouldn't really be stealing. We'd just be borrowing the car for a little while."

"I'm not going to let you steal a car," Colin insisted. "I draw the line at breaking the law."

"And just how are we going to get a car?" she asked, brushing a stray strand of dusty hair out of her eyes. "We've got two hundred dollars left."

He stared down at her grimy face. Even when she was covered with dust and perspiration, Isabelle Channing managed to look incredibly sexy. "And we still have the watch and the ring."

"There isn't a car in this town worth as much as either that watch or my ring. And I haven't seen a pawnshop around, either. Besides, we might need the ring and watch. Do you know offhand how much a Mexican divorce costs?"

"Where did you learn to steal cars?" he asked, deftly changing the subject as he grabbed her hand and tugged her in another direction.

"Tony Silva taught me. We dated in high school. He was a juvenile delinquent and an aspiring criminal. My mother hated him, so I refused to stop dating him. I can also pick a lock and jimmy a door if need be." She turned and started back toward the lot. "Come on, let's see what they have here. I'm really good with Pontiacs and Oldsmobiles. Chevys give me problems."

He stopped short. "We cannot steal a car!"

Isabelle dropped her bags to the ground, where they landed in a puff of dust. She hitched her hands on her waist and leveled her gaze on him. "We just spent the past hour and a half walking along a deserted highway. Three cars and two trucks went by and no one picked us up. Hitchhiking doesn't look like an option. And I don't think Greyhound travels this route. We can also rule out Amtrak and all major airlines. We're almost out of money, chief, so our choices are limited."

"It's against the law," he insisted.

"We'll bring it back just as soon as we're finished with it."

"No," Colin said. "I won't let you do this."

"Then you can walk to Tijuana while I drive." She strode toward the first car in line and yanked the door open. To Colin's dismay, it was unlocked. Isabelle cocked her head toward the road. "You better start now. You've got a long way to go. And I wouldn't want you to be witness to a felony."

Colin's patience had reached an end. In a few long strides, he crossed the lot and grabbed her arm, then slammed the car door. "I saved your butt out in the desert. I'm not about to let you rot in some jail. We're going to get a room at the motel, get some dinner and review our options—our lawful options."

She snatched up her belongings. "I'm not giving

up my diamond ring for some clunker of a car," she muttered as she stalked past him toward the motel, her bags bouncing against her hips.

"It's not *your* diamond ring," Colin shouted. "That ring is community property."

"Just try to get it off my finger."

Colin leaned back against the battered hood of the car and shook his head. This whole thing was getting way out of hand. He didn't want to be married to Isabelle Channing, yet at every turn, he found himself thinking of her as his wife! And if he wasn't mistaken, she was enjoying their little "marriage." She'd certainly adapted well to the role of the shrewish housewife.

He tipped his head back and let out a long breath. He hadn't thought about Maggie Kelley in...in what seemed like days. His life with her was just a dim memory. Isabelle had that effect. When he looked at her, it was like looking into the sun—she seemed to blot out all other women, from his mind, from his life.

It was becoming more and more apparent he wasn't going to marry Maggie. He didn't love her and whether she accepted that fact or not, he wasn't willing to enter into a passionless marriage. So once he got his divorce, he'd return to Chicago, break up with Maggie and get on with his life.

He glanced down at his watch. Less than twenty-four hours ago, he'd walked out of the Spencer Center and right into this mess. He'd thought the new millennium would bring order to his life, but instead he was caught in the midst of chaos—standing in the middle of nowhere, contemplating stealing a car with a woman he both detested and desired at the same time.

Colin shook his head, then straightened. Though he didn't want to admit it, he was having a good time. He'd never gambled before, never visited the Hoover Dam, never been held at gunpoint. He'd experienced more with Isabelle Channing in the past day than he'd experienced in his entire adult life. Maybe she was right, maybe he just needed to relax and enjoy the ride—even if it was in a stolen car.

He slowly walked across the parking lot toward the motel. All around him, the sky had turned a deep violet blue. The sun had dropped below the horizon and the first stars twinkled in the high desert sky. The air was clean and crisp and somewhere in the distance a coyote howled. This wasn't a bad place to spend the first day of the new millennium, he mused. And the truth be told, he couldn't think of anyone he'd rather be with in this godforsaken backwater than Isabelle Channing.

By the time he reached the motel, Isabelle had parked herself and her shopping bags on an old bench next to the office door. She'd purchased a root beer from a nearby vending machine and was casually sipping it. "I got a room," she said as he approached.

"Just one?"

"We can only afford one. Besides, we're married. I'm sure we can share a motel room without getting carried away. I have the distinct feeling the magic has already left our relationship."

"Either you don't have a very high opinion of marriage or you don't have a high opinion of me. Which is it?"

The question made her squirm and she lowered her eyes and pretended to study the soda bottle. "The room was twenty nine dollars, which leaves us with a balance of a hundred and seventy-one in cash. We can afford to spend twenty one dollars on dinner. The motel manager says the roadhouse on the other side of the highway serves pretty good burgers."

Colin grabbed her bags along with his own. "Sounds good." He followed her down the canopied sidewalk to room 7, then waited as she slipped the key into the lock. When the door swung open, he got a good look at where the two of them would be spending the night.

It wasn't quite the High Rollers Suite they'd shared at the hotel in Las Vegas. A double bed with a definite dip in the middle dominated the tiny room. The furnishings dated back to the early sixties with a Formica table and two vinyl covered chairs arranged near the window. Some tacky pictures decorated the room and, as he stepped inside, he noticed everything was bolted to the walls, including the television.

Suddenly, he didn't feel very hungry. All he really wanted to do was crawl into bed and fall asleep. But Colin knew there wouldn't be much sleeping tonight with Isabelle in the same room. Even if they didn't share a bed, he'd be forced to watch her in various states of undress, forced to cool the desire that seemed to overtake him every time she was near. With a soft sigh, he tossed the bags on the bed and it creaked in protest. "So this is what twenty-nine dollars buys in Skull Creek, California," he murmured.

Isabelle smiled, the simple act instantly breaking

the tension between them. "You're slumming now. Look, the bed vibrates. You have a quarter?"

"I thought we were on the budget plan," he said.

"Come on," Isabelle insisted. "Let's give it a try."

He reached in his pocket, withdrew a quarter and tossed it to her. She plugged it into the machine beside the bed, then hopped onto the creaky mattress, stretching out in front of him like a temptress, one arm resting along her hip, her head braced by her bent elbow.

Colin's gaze drifted along her body, from her pretty toes displayed by the sandals he'd bought her, along her slender legs, to the sweet curve of her hip. His fingers clenched as he remembered how easily his hands spanned her waist, how delicate she felt beneath his touch.

The bed began to vibrate and Isabelle giggled, flopping over on her back and throwing her arms out on either side of her. The creaking that accompanied the vibrations was enough to render any effort at relaxation completely useless. "Come on," she said. "Try it out. It's really quite…invigorating."

Reluctantly, Colin sat down on the opposite side of the bed. She grabbed his arm and tugged him down beside her. For a long time, they lay side by side, staring at the ceiling, their fingers laced between them. He wasn't sure what was going through Isabelle's mind, but Colin couldn't help but wonder what had happened the last time they shared a bed.

She had obviously wanted to make love with him that night after their wedding. What was stopping them from enjoying the same pleasures in this bed? If he turned to her and kissed her, would she respond?

Or would the action simply cause another one of their all-too-familiar arguments?

He rolled to his side and pushed up on his elbow, staring down at Isabelle's beautiful features. She had closed her eyes and a tiny smile curled the corners of her mouth. He wanted to taste that mouth again, to linger longer than he had the last time, to see where one perfect kiss might lead. Slowly, Colin leaned closer, stopping when his mouth hovered over hers.

Isabelle opened her eyes and met his gaze. They watched each other for a moment, wary, neither one of them anxious to make the first move. He felt her breath warm on his lips and he heard her sigh softly. "This bed is very...relaxing," she murmured.

He closed his eyes, ready to cover her mouth with his. At that moment the bed stopped vibrating. The room fell silent and in the blink of an eye, reality suddenly returned to room 7 of the Skull Creek Motorlodge.

He had to stop kissing Isabelle Channing! Though the woman was his wife, there couldn't be any romantic feelings between them. They were going to get a divorce as soon as they got to Mexico and then he'd put this whole sordid mess behind him. Kissing her and touching her and fantasizing about what they might share wouldn't do either one of them any good.

"I—I'm sorry," he said, drawing away. "I—I didn't mean to—it was just the bed."

"Hmm. Who would have thought you could have so much fun for only a quarter?" she murmured, her sultry gaze fixed on his mouth.

She wanted to be kissed right then. Colin could see it in her eyes, in the way her lips quivered slightly as she spoke, in the way she held her breath. What harm could one little kiss do? After all, they were married. Husbands kissed their wives all the time, didn't they? He drew a deep breath, anticipating the taste of her.

But then, Isabelle moaned softly and sat up. She ran her fingers through her hair and smoothed her skirt with her palms. "I'm hungry. Maybe we should go get something to eat. There's got to be more fun in this town than a vibrating bed."

As she stood up, Colin's eyes lingered a bit longer on her backside. He wondered if she wore the panties he'd bought for her in Las Vegas. Though he'd told her the saleslady had picked them out, in truth, Colin had final say on the choices of lingerie. She probably looked incredibly sexy beneath that dress, wearing a few scraps of black lace and silk.

Colin swallowed. Or maybe she wasn't wearing any underwear at all. Just the possibility sent a new flood of desire racing through his bloodstream. He could reach out and unbutton her dress and then he'd lose himself in her body and before long—

"Are you coming?"

Her question snapped him back to reality once again and, for a moment, he wasn't sure what she meant. "What?"

Isabelle stood at the door. "To dinner. Are you coming to dinner or are you going to lie on that bed for the rest of the night?"

Chagrined, Colin jumped to his feet and nodded. "Of course. Dinner. Dinner would be fine." He drew a ragged breath and watched as Isabelle stepped outside. Then he moved toward the door, taking a long look around the motel room.

"Maybe I should have let her steal the car," he muttered. "At least I wouldn't have to risk spending the night here."

THE MILLENNIUM festivities at the Happy Jackrabbit Saloon were in full swing when Isabelle and Colin walked in the door. As soon as Colin got a look at the clientele, he grabbed Isabelle firmly around the waist and put himself between her and the more disreputable-looking patrons. For a moment, he felt her stiffen beside him, but then she relaxed and allowed him to guide her through the bar to the tables near the back.

They found an empty booth and settled in. A few minutes later, a waitress dressed in a skintight T-shirt and a minuscule skirt dropped a few menus in front of them. Though most of the other men in the place would have given the woman's cleavage a good study, compared to Isabelle, she didn't deserve a second look.

"You here for the contest?" she asked, directing her question to Isabelle and snapping her gum at the same time.

"Contest?"

"If you're enterin' the contest, you get to eat free."

"Both of us?" Isabelle asked.

The waitress shook her head. "Nope. Just you."

Isabelle smiled, then shot him a questioning look. "Sure, I'll enter the contest. What's the prize if I win?"

"Two thousand," the waitress said. "Biggest prize all year on account of the millennium."

Isabelle's eyes went wide and she turned to Colin. "Two thousand dollars?" She glanced around the room, then leaned over to Colin. "I know I'm smarter than most of the people here. We could buy a nice car for two thousand dollars."

"This ain't a contest of brains, honey," the waitress said. "It's more a contest of boobs."

"It's for stupid people?" Colin asked.

The waitress looked at him as if he'd just sprouted horns. "No, it's a wet T-shirt contest. Now, do you folks want something to drink or not?"

He watched as Isabelle stifled a laugh at his naiveté, then turned back to the waitress and ordered a beer, even though he didn't drink. Somehow, a beer seemed the proper thing to drink in a place like the Happy Jackrabbit. Isabelle requested a club soda and when the waitress finally walked away with their dinner order, he already knew what Isabelle had in mind. He decided to stop the argument before it even started. "No wife of mine is going to enter a wet T-shirt contest," he said. "End of discussion."

Though he may have stopped talking about it, he couldn't help but imagine the possibilities. Isabelle's body combined with soaking-wet and slightly transparent cotton proved to be a tantalizing image. And she was probably a wonderful dancer, lithe and sinuous and provocative.

"And why not?" she asked, her eyes narrowing. "It's perfectly legal. Unlike stealing a car, this wouldn't be breaking the law. And you said we needed to consider our lawful options."

Colin banished the erotic images from his head. "Isabelle, nothing you say is going to make me change my mind. I might be able to defend you against an old lady with a fake handgun. But look at this place. Most of these guys could bench-press a

Buick. And I think the tooth-to-tattoo rule is in effect here." He glanced around. "The number of tattoos on a guy's body is in direct proportion to the number of teeth he's lost in bar fights. I prefer to keep all my teeth."

"It's just a little contest," Isabelle said. "I'll be wearing a T-shirt. What's the big deal?" She glanced down. "Don't you think I have nice breasts?"

Colin swallowed hard. Now there's a question he could answer without thinking. He'd been ruminating on her breasts quite a lot lately and he thought they were pretty much the most perfect breasts he'd ever come across. "I think you have very lovely...breasts," he said.

"Lovely enough to win two thousand dollars?"

She was challenging him again and doing a damn fine job of it. Hell, yes, she could probably win a few million with that body of hers. But he wasn't about to tell her that. "You're not going to enter the contest," he repeated, his voice deceptively calm.

"Do you know how those words make me feel?"

The waitress brought their drinks and Colin immediately took a deep swallow of his beer. He licked the foam from his upper lip, then met her defiant gaze. "I know exactly how those words make you feel. You hate it when I order you around. You feel compelled to do the exact opposite. If I had suggested you enter the contest, you would have accused me of being a pig." He leaned back and stretched his arm over the back of the booth. "We don't need the money. I told you, we still have my watch and the ring."

"I can enter the contest if I want to," she said.

He leaned forward, bracing his arms on the table.

"And you could have stolen that car, if you really wanted to. Sometimes I think you do and say these things just to see what kind of reaction you'll get from me," Colin said. He raised his eyebrow and sent her a shrewd look. "Am I right? Is this another one of your tests?"

With a soft oath, Isabelle guzzled down her club soda, stood up and slid out of the booth. "When my food comes, have the waitress wrap it up. I'm going back to the motel. I've lost my appetite."

He watched her weave her way back to the front door. She deftly avoided groping hands and lewd comments and Colin made sure no one had followed her out before he sank back into the booth. "I'm getting better at this marriage thing all the time," he muttered.

At least she was starting to listen to him. Although Colin knew Isabelle didn't need him to watch out for her, he couldn't help himself. For all her street smarts and innate intelligence, she was surprisingly reckless. She was legally his wife and he wasn't going to turn a blind eye to her antics—at least not for the few days they were married.

He took another sip of beer. Hell, he'd love to see Isabelle in a wet T-shirt. But if she entered the contest, all the other men in the Happy Jackrabbit would enjoy a sight that Colin believed was his and his alone. There were certain conventions in marriage that a guy had to respect. And though Isabelle would be his wife for only a few days, he was determined to stick to the rules. Hell, there had to be a rule about a wife prancing around half-naked in front of a crowd of drunken cowboys.

His mind flashed another image of her, wet cotton

clinging to the supple curves of her breasts, nipples hardened to tantalizing peaks. He drained his mug of beer, then motioned for the waitress to bring him another. A long howl sounded over the saloon's sound system and he turned to see an enormous man standing on a stage at the far end of the bar.

"All right, boys! The fun's about to begin. My name's Leroy and I own this joint, so you better behave yerselfs or I'll personally crack yer heads. We've got some pretty little gals up here and a bucket of cold water for each of them. Our big Millennium Wet T-Shirt Contest is about to begin!"

A round of hoots and hollers erupted from the audience. Colin leaned back in his seat. He'd never been in a place quite like the Happy Jackrabbit. He usually preferred a more upscale spot with a refined clientele. A place where the bartenders didn't look like professional wrestlers and where the waitresses didn't fall out of their outfits.

Colin looked up to see his very own waitress standing next to the booth. She dropped a plate in front of him, then nodded at Isabelle's empty spot. "You want me to take this back to the kitchen? I can keep it warm till she's through."

Colin frowned. "She's not in the bathroom."

"Naw, I meant the contest."

"She went back to the motel," Colin explained.

"I just saw her backstage," the waitress said.

"No, she went back to the motel," Colin insisted. "You must be mistaken. Just wrap up her meal and I'll take it with me."

The waitress shrugged and retreated with Isabelle's dinner. Colin nearly called her back to ask her to do the same for his meal, determined to make sure

Isabelle really had returned to the room. But then he changed his mind and decided to eat in. Isabelle had her moments, but she was certainly sensible enough not to cross him on this subject. Entering a wet T-shirt contest was beyond what even Isabelle Channing would do on a dare.

"Yeah, I'm getting much better at this marriage business," he said with a self-satisfied smile.

6

ISABELLE STOOD near the edge of the stage with nine other contestants of varying shapes and sizes. Since she'd worn a dress to the Happy Jackrabbit, she'd been provided with a T-shirt bearing the saloon's emblem, a grinning, gap-toothed hare with a beer mug in his paw. As for the rest of her outfit, she had to make do with the black panties and shoes Colin had purchased for her in Las Vegas.

In all honesty, she was more conservatively dressed than she usually was on the beach. Though the T-shirt was tight, it wasn't completely transparent and her panties covered all the most critical parts. She wasn't really worried about her wardrobe. She was worried about Colin's reaction.

That's what this was all about, wasn't it? She knew they didn't need the money to make it to Mexico—they had the watch and her ring. She was simply using that as an excuse to push the boundaries with him, to prove she wouldn't let any man, not even her husband, dictate the terms of her day-to-day life. And this was a perfect way to illustrate that point. If she wanted to stand in front of a bunch of drunkards and show off her own body, then that was her right, wasn't it?

And this was certain to push Colin over the edge. After he saw her onstage, he wouldn't want to kiss her anymore or do sweet things for her. He wouldn't look into her eyes the way he did, those looks that made her breath catch in her throat and her heart do little flip-flops. Isabelle closed her eyes and tried to gather her determination.

This had to do it. All the arguing hadn't. Nor had the detour to the Hoover Dam or Edith. Every time she turned around, Colin Spencer was revealing himself as a man she could truly love. He was caring and loyal and considerate.

But she couldn't love Colin! That wasn't in the plan. Twenty-four hours ago, they'd been trapped together in an elevator. Chance had taken them down to the lobby instead of back up to the party. If things had gone differently, she might be at home right now, nursing a champagne hangover, instead of wearing a skimpy T-shirt waiting to get drenched with a bucket of cold water.

The emcee, a hulk of a man named Leroy, announced the contest and she pasted a smile on her face as she watched the guy with the bucket approach. One by one, he doused the girls in line ahead of her, each of them letting out a little scream. When he reached her spot with a full bucket, Isabelle held her nose and closed her eyes.

She didn't expect the water to be quite so cold, and when it hit her full force, she gasped. Before she could open her eyes, she felt someone grab her around the waist and lift her off her feet. Instinctively, she lashed out, catching her captor in the cheek with her elbow.

"Damn it, Isabelle, I should have known you'd try something like this."

A maelstrom of emotion shot through her—anger,

surprise, relief. Isabelle wasn't sure which one she felt the most. Embarrassment came to mind as Colin tossed her over his shoulder and wrapped his arms around her legs. With no care for her dignity, he lugged her through the main room of the saloon. One of the girls from the contest hurried after them with Isabelle's dress and sweater. The audience whooped encouragement, calling out bawdy suggestions as Isabelle's hair dribbled water across the floor.

"Put me down!" she cried, beating him on the back with her wadded-up dress.

"Not a chance."

She tried to wriggle out of his grasp, but he only held on tighter. As he passed their table, the waitress handed him a brown paper bag and he tucked it under his arm, then headed for the front door. When they made it outside, the crisp night air hit the wet fabric of her T-shirt and she began to shiver. "You— you can put me down now," she demanded through chattering teeth.

He wasn't in the mood to listen and started across the parking lot. When they reached the highway, he looked both ways, then jogged across, his shoulder jabbing into her belly until she couldn't breathe. Colin didn't put her down even when they got to the door of their motel room.

"Where's the key?"

With a vivid oath, Isabelle reached into the pocket of her dress, pulled it out and handed it to him beneath his arm. This was humiliating, being carried around like some Neanderthal's conquest! Next thing, he'd throw her down on the bed and ravish her.

Colin kicked open the door to the room, crossed to

the bed and tossed her onto the creaky mattress. She waited, her temper piqued, her hair hanging down over her eyes. But he didn't choose to ravish her. Instead, he stood above her, his expression filled with unrestrained fury. He opened his mouth to say something, then thought better of it and merely ran his hand through his hair, cursing beneath his breath. When he'd finally calmed himself, he leveled his gaze on her. "What the hell were you trying to prove?"

"I could ask the same of you," she retorted, shoving her wet hair out of her eyes.

He slowly shook his head. "I thought by now we would have come to some kind of understanding between us. I know you don't particularly care for me, but at least we could respect each other's feelings."

This time, Isabelle opened her mouth and snapped it shut before speaking. His anger had softened to what looked like disappointment, and a flood of remorse rushed through her. What was wrong with her? She should be happy someone like Colin bothered to care for her, enough to ride in like some white knight every time she got herself in trouble.

"Then you should respect me," she said, pushing up off the bed. "I can make my own decisions, and if I want to enter that contest, I can."

She made for the door, but he grabbed her arm and yanked her around. Isabelle tried to struggle out of his grasp, but he managed to get hold of her other arm, pulling her hard against his body. "You're not going back there," he warned.

"You can't stop me," she said.

He stared down at her, their gazes locked for a long moment. And then Isabelle saw something that caused a shiver to run down her spine. His anger had slowly dissolved into undisguised desire.

A groan slipped from his throat. He lowered his mouth to hers and without any hesitation, he kissed her. His lips were hard and demanding and Isabelle fought back, meeting his desire with her own, refusing to relinquish her own anger. Her mind screamed a warning. If she couldn't control her own desire, how could she control him?

When her head began to swim, Isabelle thought of how he'd bullied her. And when her knees went weak, she told herself he meant nothing to her. But when he gently pushed her back toward the bed, she couldn't think at all.

They tumbled onto the bed together, the mattress shrieking beneath them. But it wasn't enough to squelch the passion building between them. He stretched his body over hers, bracing his hands on either side of her head, yet never breaking contact with her mouth, keeping her a virtual prisoner with his kisses.

The weight of him, the hard muscle and lean limbs, felt good against her body and the wet T-shirt she wore was like a second skin, arousing sensations she fought hard to ignore. Possession slowly turned to seduction as his mouth traced a line from her jaw to her shoulder. He pulled back the T-shirt and bit her gently.

"I hate you," Isabelle murmured, tilting her head until he found a wonderfully sensitive spot.

"And I hate you," he replied, his breath hot on her cool skin.

Colin's hands skimmed up along her rib cage until his palms cupped her breasts. Her body betrayed her as a wild current of desire sparked every nerve she possessed. When his fingers toyed at her hardened nipples, she lost the ability to breathe. Isabelle cried out, arching against him.

"I really, really...hate you," he murmured, his words soft and urgent.

Her breath came in short gasps. "But I hate you more," she countered.

With a low groan, he grabbed her face between his hands then rolled her over on top of him, molding his mouth to hers, kissing her until all rational thought evaporated from her brain and she was left with only raw hunger.

Isabelle straddled his waist and reached for the buttons of his shirt, then frantically worked them open with trembling fingers. His shirt parted and she bent down to press her mouth to the base of his throat. She felt his pulse beat hard and fast beneath her lips and she knew he wanted her as much as she wanted him.

Rocking back on her heels, Isabelle stared down into his passion-glazed eyes. His arousal, evident through the fabric of his pants, was hard between her legs. With a devilish smile, she shifted slightly and he sucked in a sharp breath, closing his eyes, both pain and pleasure coloring his expression.

How could this be so right and yet so wrong at the same time? She wanted him to make love with her, she wanted to forget that so much stood between them. This didn't have to make sense, did it? Isabelle sighed softly, then leaned over and pressed her forehead against his.

He slowly opened his eyes and furrowed his fingers through her hair, stealing another furtive kiss. "Oh, Isabelle. What are we doing here?"

She brushed her mouth against his, teasing, then pulling away. "Do you want me?"

"I want you," he murmured, kissing her again, deep and hard. "I want you." He grazed her lower lip with his teeth. "I want you." His tongue touched hers in a slow, delicious meeting. "I love you, Isabelle," he murmured, the words disappearing into his kiss.

"I love you, too," Isabelle said, the sentiment slipping from her lips like a sigh.

She realized what she had said at just about the same instant Colin realized what *he* had said. From fast forward to full reverse, their passion ground to a halt and the breath slowly left Isabelle's body. She stared down at him, blinking in surprise, not sure what to say at such a time.

"I—I—" No matter how hard she tried to put a coherent thought together, her mind refused to work. She scrambled off him, then stood beside the bed, shifting from foot to foot. "We—I mean, that wasn't—"

He held out his hand to stop her explanation. "It was my fault."

"No, no," Isabelle said. "I think it was my fault."

Colin levered himself up from the bed, taking a spot on the opposite side. He quickly rebuttoned his shirt and tucked it neatly into his pants. Then, with a long sigh, he ran his fingers through his hair. He glanced over at her and forced a smile. "I should go," he said.

"Go?" Isabelle frowned. "Where?"

"I—I—" He pressed his lips together and cleared

his throat. "Back to the Happy Jackrabbit," he replied. "I still owe the waitress for our dinners." He turned around and began to search the room, finally finding her dress in a heap beside the door. "I'll just take some money," he said, retrieving the wad of cash from her pocket and holding it out in front of him.

Isabelle nodded and she watched as he withdrew a few bills. When he took what he needed, he neatly folded her dress and put it on the table in front of the window. Then he risked another glance at her.

"Maybe you should change out of that wet T-shirt," he mumbled. "I—I wouldn't want you to catch...cold."

Isabelle looked down to see her nipples poking at the damp fabric. She crossed her arms over her chest and felt a warm blush work its way up her cheeks.

Colin shrugged, then turned and yanked open the door. He slipped out of the room as fast as he could without actually running, Isabelle mused. And when she was all alone, she sat down at the edge of the bed and twisted out of the T-shirt. Accompanied by a string of disparaging remarks on his character, Isabelle flung the T-shirt at the door. It hit the wall beside the window with a splat, then dropped to the floor.

She flopped back on the bed and covered her eyes with her hands. "Why can't you be like most wives?" she cried. "They manage to avoid sex all the time. I have a headache. I've had a long day. Don't you ever get enough? We just had sex last night." She frowned. "No, that one wouldn't work."

Isabelle ran a litany of excuses through her mind, but as she chose a few of the most plausible, she realized she didn't want to avoid sex with Colin Spencer. In fact, she wanted to have sex with him as much and as often as she could. She craved his kisses and hungered for the feel of his body on top of hers.

She just didn't want to love him!

COLIN FOUND a spot at the bar and slid onto a stool between a grizzled old cowboy wearing a battered leather vest and a middle-aged woman in a spangly western shirt and painfully tight jeans. He tossed some money on the bar and the emcee from the wet T-shirt contest, an enormous bearded man with a "Mother" tattoo on his arm, lumbered up to him. His name was Elroy—or maybe it was Leroy.

"Give me a beer," Colin said.

"I shouldn't serve you," the bartender muttered. "You can't go hauling my contestants out before they've had a chance to strut their stuff. It's not good for business."

Colin sighed. Maybe he ought to leave right away. Considering Leroy's size and temperament, he could pretty much count on a fist to the face sooner or later. It seemed that Isabelle could cause problems even when she wasn't in the room. "My wife has a tendency to misbehave," he said. "And she likes to irritate me. It's my responsibility to keep her in line."

"Yer wife?" The man chuckled and slid a beer in front of Colin. "I 'spose I can't argue with that. I'm not sure I'd want my old lady displayin' her assets in front of the rowdies in this bar. But I have to say, that little gal of yours was the odds-on favorite once the T-shirts were all soaked. You could have been a couple thousand richer if you'd let her compete." He wiped his hands on a bar rag, then held out his palm. "Leroy Harbison. I own this joint."

Colin shook his hand. "Colin Spencer. Nice to meet you, Leroy."

Leroy wiped down the bar in front of Colin as he studied him shrewdly. "You ain't from around these parts, are you?"

Colin picked a peanut out of a bowl beside him and cracked it open. "We're just passing through and we ran into a little…car trouble. Say, do you know anyplace in town we can rent a car?"

"Rent a car?" This brought a loud guffaw from Leroy, his palm cracking against the scarred wooden bar. "Well, Colin, we've been pleadin' with Hertz to set up an office here in Skull Creek, but they ain't got back to us yet. They said they're waitin' for us to put in our international airport." He shook his head. "Geez, you city folks are a laugh riot. Where do you think you are, Los Angeles?"

Colin leaned forward, his elbows braced against the brass railing surrounding the bar. "Listen, I have to get to Mexico and we got carjacked by some crazy old lady on the highway north of here. I have to find a car."

"You on the run from the law?" Leroy asked.

Colin shook his head. "No."

"Then what's so urgent?"

When he didn't answer, the bartender poured a shot of tequila and set it on the bar next to Colin's mug of beer. "Drink it," he said. "Whatever problems you got will be a lot easier to handle after a shot or two."

Colin pushed the shot glass away. "I'm really not

much of a drinker. The last time I got drunk, I accidentally married my fiancée's best friend."

Leroy shook his head and pushed the glass back toward him. "Man, you do have problems." He poured a shot for himself, then held it up. "Here's to women. Can't live with them, can't run 'em over with your truck, either."

Reluctantly, Colin picked up his glass and touched it to Leroy's, then swallowed the shot in one gulp. The liquor burned a trail of fire down his throat. After the initial inferno, a warm sensation settled into his chest. In truth, the tequila cleared his head and dulled his confusion.

"It's not that I don't like her," Colin explained. "I mean, she's a helluva woman. Smart, sexy, and she has this mouth—"

Leroy nodded and winked. "The kind you could lose yourself in, eh?"

Colin frowned, then cleared his throat. "Well, yeah. Maybe. Definitely." He took a sip of beer. "But that's not what I meant. I meant, she has a way with words."

"Ah, sharp-tongued. A real nag. Those are the worst. My third wife was like that," Leroy said. "We'd get in a fight and I'd come out feeling like I'd been beat with a bullwhip. Boy, was I glad when she ran off with the circus."

"Your wife ran off with the circus?"

"It was really the carnival. They were driving through town and stopped here for dinner. She took off with the guy who ran the Ferris wheel."

"Women," Colin said, shaking his head.

"I got just the thing to take yer mind off yer troubles," Leroy said. "Me and the boys, we got a regular poker game going in the back room. Starts in a couple minutes. Yer welcome to join us if you like."

Colin held up his hand. "Nah, I'm not much for gambling. I lost my shirt in Vegas."

"It's just a friendly game of poker," Leroy said. "And we love to have amateurs sit in. Makes the game more interesting."

"I don't have much money."

"It don't take much," Leroy insisted. He grabbed the bottle of tequila and their empty shot glasses, and yelled a few instructions to the other bartenders. Then he nodded to Colin and started off toward the rear of the roadhouse. At first, Colin was going to refuse. Hell, what did he know about cards? But Leroy wasn't the kind of man who took no for an answer. And Colin did want to take his mind off Isabelle, at least for a little while.

As they walked past the stage, an image of her flashed in his brain, searing away the effects of the tequila. His fingers tingled and he could still feel her body beneath his hands, the warm swell of her breasts, the sweet curve of her hips. A knot of desire tightened in his gut and he groaned inwardly as he recalled Leroy's comment about her mouth.

Why hadn't he stayed? With a little effort, they might have been able to pick up where they left off. Right now, they could be tangled in the sheets, naked and flushed with passion, her body arching beneath his as he brought them both to a climax neither one of them would forget.

It was all going so well...until he told her he loved her. Colin rubbed the back of his neck. The words had just popped out. He didn't know where they'd come from or what they really meant. He couldn't possibly love Isabelle Channing! They barely knew each other. Besides that, she drove him stark raving mad.

But how was he supposed to know what love was all about? In truth, he'd never been in love before. He knew now he hadn't loved Maggie Kelley. But he couldn't say for certain that he didn't love Isabelle Channing. There was something about her that defied all logic and rational thought. She was an exciting woman, a woman who brought out a side of him he didn't know he possessed—a passionate, reckless side.

"Are you comin'?"

Startled out of his thoughts, Colin glanced up to see Leroy waiting for him. "Yeah, I'm coming."

The back room was little more than a storage closet with a felt-covered table set in the middle. He took a chair next to Leroy and smiled while he was introduced to the rest of the boys. There was Darnell, Leroy's large cousin. And Leroy's other cousin, Euby, who outweighed them both by about fifty pounds. The quintet was completed by a rangy cowboy named Breezy.

Colin knew the basics of poker, but as the first hand was dealt, Leroy gave him a quick overview. Ten-dollar ante, ten-dollar raise, three raise limit. Jacks or better to open. Five card draw, nothing's wild. He scrambled to make sense of the instructions, then tossed in a ten-dollar bill into the center of the table when everyone else did.

He lost his first hand with a dismal pair of threes. After that, his luck began to turn as he started to get the hang of the game. After all his experience in negotiating high-stakes business deals, he found he was a natural at bluffing. The money began to pile up until his luck turned and he lost most of it to Darnell.

As they played, they chatted about sports and work. As the pitchers of beer disappeared, the talk turned back to women—most notably, Colin's woman.

"I bet she's one of them modern women," Leroy said. "What do they call themselves?"

"Feminists?" Colin said.

"Yeah, that's it. She expects you to pick up yer socks and take out the garbage and put the toilet seat down."

"Well, I don't really know," Colin said. "I've never lived with her. We just got married on New Year's Eve. We haven't had a chance to get to know each other very well."

"Plenty of time for that," Leroy said.

"Not really. We're going to get a divorce. That's why we're on our way to Mexico."

"Ooo, whee," Darnell said. "She must be pretty bad fer you to divorce her that quick. I thought Leroy held the record on the shortest marriage. One of his lasted three weeks."

Colin shook his head, then asked the dealer for three cards. "I don't know. Marriage isn't that bad. I'm kind of enjoying myself." He studied his cards and when the bet came around to him, he tossed in another ten.

"Good sex, eh?" Leroy said.

"Actually, we haven't had sex. At least not that I can remember. And not that it would make any difference. I mean, I love Isabelle for who she—"

"You love her?" Leroy asked.

Colin winced, then tossed down his cards and

rubbed his eyes. "Did I say that again?" He drew a deep breath and sighed. "Why do I keep saying that? I don't want to say it, but it keeps slipping out. It must be the beer."

"Yeah, right," Leroy said. "Blame it on the beer."

The game went on until way past closing time, his fortunes rising and falling with the deal of the cards. Colin thought it best to keep his wits about him, to avoid any off-the-cuff proclamations, so he drank far less beer than his companions. By the time they called an end to the game, he was up three hundred dollars.

Everyone pushed back from the table, but as they grumbled about their losses, Colin grabbed his stack of bills and threw it into the center of the table. "I need a vehicle," he announced. His watch followed, plopping down on top of the cash. "That's an expensive watch. It's worth a couple thousand. Any of you gents have a car you'd be willing to ante up? I'll play you one hand."

The men glanced at each other, then at the cash and jewelry in the center of the table. Leroy pulled out his chair and sat back down. "I've got me a pickup truck," he said. "An '83 Ford with a hundred and fifty thousand miles. Had the tranny rebuilt just last year. She runs great, but I don't think she's worth what you're bettin'."

Colin leaned back in his chair, ruffling the deck of cards between his fingers. "That doesn't make any difference. If you've got a truck, then we've got a game. And the game is five card draw, best hand takes it all."

He shuffled the cards and then dealt ten between the two of them. As he picked up his hand, he wasn't sure whether he wanted to win or lose. Winning a truck meant he and Isabelle could be on their way to Mexico to get their divorce. Losing might mean another night at the Skull Creek Motorlodge, one more chance to see what might happen if they spent the night together in the same room.

He slowly fanned out his cards in front of him, remembering the gamble he'd taken on the elevator. If it had gone up, he would have married Maggie Kelley. But it had gone down and now he was married to Isabelle Channing. He closed his eyes, reluctant to look down at his cards.

If he thought that first gamble was a risk, this was even bigger. Because this time, he was risking his entire future.

WHEN ISABELLE WOKE the next morning, she was alone. The other side of the bed hadn't been slept in and she noticed her Happy Jackrabbit T-shirt was still sitting in front of the door. Colin had gone out and hadn't returned.

Her first thought was that he'd deserted her, leaving her to fend for herself in Skull Creek. But she immediately ruled that idea out. Colin would never just walk away. He took his responsibilities as a husband—at least those outside the marital bed—very seriously.

Her mind wandered back to the night before. They'd come so close. She wasn't sure whether she was relieved or disappointed they had stopped when they did. Isabelle had never lost control as she had with Colin. There had been other men in her life, but always on her own terms. Sex had been interesting, even mildly exciting, but never overwhelming. Colin made her feel powerless to resist him.

She rolled over on her stomach and pulled the pillow over her head. His words ran through her mind and she replayed them over and over again. *I love you, Isabelle.*

At least *she* knew what he meant. Men had always had trouble differentiating between love and desire. "I love you" really meant "I want to make love to you." It didn't have anything to do with emotion, Isabelle reassured herself. Colin wanted her body, not her heart and soul. A man like Colin wasn't capable of real love.

Isabelle rolled out of bed and padded to the bathroom. When she saw her reflection in the mirror, she groaned. Going to bed with wet hair made for a serious case of bedhead in the morning.

She quickly showered and dressed, then dragged a comb through her damp, tangled hair. When she opened the door of the motel room, the bright midmorning light hit her eyes and she squinted. A battered pickup truck was parked right outside the room, and as she looked through the opened window of the driver's-side door she saw Colin stretched across the front seat, his eyes closed.

She stepped up on the rusty running board and stuck her head in the window. For a moment, she thought about letting him sleep. He looked exhausted, his arm thrown over his head at an uncomfortable angle. His hair stood up in errant spikes and a purple bruise marred his right cheekbone.

"Colin?" He didn't open his eyes and she reached into the truck and shook his foot. "Colin!"

His eyes snapped open and he held his hand up to

block the glare of the sun streaming through the windshield, wincing as if he was in pain. When he saw her, he groaned and threw his arm back over his eyes. "Go away," he murmured.

She smiled. He looked awfully handsome in the morning, all rumpled and sleepy and undeniably sexy. A rough stubble darkened his angled jaw. He looked like the kind of man she could drag back into bed for the rest of the morning. "Did you sleep out here all night?"

"Not all night. Just since about three in the morning."

"Don't you think you'd better get out of this truck before the owner catches you?"

"I am the owner," he murmured, rolling over on his side and trying to get more comfortable.

"This is your truck?" she asked.

"I won it. In an after-hours poker game at the Happy Jackrabbit." He held up the paper he had clutched in his fist. "It's all legal. We now own this lovely pickup truck. Another piece of marital property."

Isabelle blinked. "I didn't know you played poker."

"I didn't, either," Colin said. "But I guess when you drink enough beer, you think you can do anything you set your mind to. Besides, it's all just a game of mathematical probabilities. Now, would you leave me alone? I have a bad headache and I need some sleep."

Isabelle stepped down from the running board and pulled the truck door open. "Come on," she said, climbing inside and grabbing his hand. With a grunt, she pulled him up to a sitting position. "Once you take a shower, you'll feel much better."

"I'll never feel better," Colin replied as he struggled out of the truck.

Isabelle draped his arm over her shoulder and helped him toward the room. He stumbled slightly and she grabbed his waist, her hand slipping up beneath the untucked tails of his shirt. When her fingers touched bare skin, a current of excitement ran through her and she stifled a moan. She gave him a sideways glance. "What happened to your eye? Did you get in a fight?"

Wincing, he reached up and touched his cheek. "You hit me," Colin said. "Last night."

"While we were...in bed?"

"No. When I carried you out of the bar. You caught me with your elbow."

Isabelle shook her head. "I don't know why you put up with me," she teased.

He chuckled. "I don't know, either. I think I must have a masochistic streak that runs very deep. This hangover is proof of that."

She maneuvered them both back into the room, then left him standing at the foot of the bed while she went into the bathroom to start the shower. When she returned, Colin had already ripped his shirt off. Her gaze slowly took in his broad shoulders and narrow waist, the perfection of his body causing her heart to stop for just an instant. She imagined her hands skimming over his skin, teasing at the faint dusting of hair running from his collarbone to his belly, skimming over the hard muscle and warm flesh. Before they'd run off to Vegas, she'd never thought of Colin Spencer as a sexual being, but half-naked, his hair mussed and his eyes sleepy, he was the sexiest man she'd ever laid eyes on. Isabelle forced a smile, then looked away.

"What?" he asked.

"Nothing," she murmured.

He wadded up his shirt in his hand and tossed it onto the bed. "I'm going to take a shower and I'd really rather do it without my clothes on. If you have a problem with that, you probably should leave."

Isabelle drew a shaky breath. "I should," she said, stepping toward the door. Just as she was about to walk outside, she glanced back to find him staring at her, his gaze intense. She didn't need to ask what was going through his mind. It was etched in his expression. "A-about last night," she began. "I really didn't—"

Colin rubbed his chest distractedly, his eyes still fixed on her face. She wanted to fall into his arms, to give herself over to the desire that had raged between them the night before, to explore every inch of his skin with her tongue. But they both stood rooted where they stood.

A careless smile curled the corners of his mouth. "Neither did I," he countered in a soft voice. "We just got carried away."

"Right," Isabelle agreed, nodding. "After all, how could we possibly..." She swallowed hard. "You know, feel that way. We barely know each other well enough to like each other, much less...you know."

"Love each other?"

There! He'd said the word she'd tried so hard to avoid. Unsaid, it seemed like such a preposterous notion. Colin Spencer in love with Isabelle Channing. And Isabelle Channing head over heels for Colin

Spencer. But hearing it aloud didn't make it any less real, or any less ridiculous.

"You should probably take that shower," she suggested. "We need to get on the road, get to Mexico, so you can get back to Chicago and marry Maggie."

Another word they'd so carefully avoided—Maggie. Isabelle had imagined what her return to Chicago might entail. She knew she'd have to explain her actions to her best friend and hope Maggie would understand. Of course, this was all predicated on the notion that Colin was the wrong man for Maggie to marry, that he was unsuited for a lifetime commitment.

But it had become blatantly clear over the past thirty-six hours that Isabelle had been wrong. Colin Spencer was a man any woman could fall in love with. After all, she had managed that little trick quite easily. Would Maggie misread her motives? Would she believe Isabelle had *stolen* Colin away for herself?

"While you take your shower, I'm going to go over to the grocery store and see if I can find some breakfast."

"Make it quick," Colin said. "I'm hoping we'll be able to get to Tijuana by this evening."

Isabelle nodded, then hurried out of the room, closing the door behind her. When she'd put solid wood between the two of them, she paused and drew a deep breath. No matter how hard she tried to put it out of her mind, she couldn't help but think she might have made a mistake with Colin and Maggie. He was a passionate man. Last night had more than proven that fact. Yet a casual observer would never attach such a description to Colin.

An image of Maggie and Colin together flashed in

her mind and a torrent of jealousy washed it away. He was Maggie's fiancé, yet he was Isabelle's husband. The only way to make it right was to divorce him. If he truly wanted to go back to Maggie, she'd have to let him go. But how could she do that if she loved him?

Isabelle pushed away from the door and headed across the parking lot. The brisk morning wind kicked up dust devils around her feet, snapping at her skirt and tangling her hair. Skull Creek, California, looked a lot seedier in the light of day than it had last night. The Happy Jackrabbit was deserted with only a few cars parked out in front. Isabelle wondered who had taken home the big two-thousand-dollar prize in last night's contest.

As she walked down the shoulder of the highway, she couldn't help but wish they could be stuck in Skull Creek just a little longer. How could a guy as bad at gambling as Colin was win a pickup truck in a poker game? What kind of luck was that? Maybe it was destiny that put transportation into his hands. Maybe they were meant to get to Mexico and get their divorce.

Isabelle turned around and stared back at the motel and at the truck that would take her to the end of her marriage. A slow smile quirked her lips as an idea came into her head. That pickup was standing between her and another day with Colin Spencer. She may not be able to handle Colin Spencer, but she could certainly take on an old truck.

"I'm trying to save my marriage," she murmured. "And all's fair in love and war."

7

"IT STARTED FINE last night," Colin said, rubbing the ache in his forehead with his fingertips. "I drove it over here, no problem."

Leroy bent under the hood and examined the engine, poking at the greasy components with a fat finger and clucking his tongue.

After his shower, Colin had decided to get gas while he waited for Isabelle to return from the store. When he tried to start the truck, the engine turned over but it wouldn't catch. He knew more about quantum physics than he did about auto mechanics, so when he saw his old buddy, Leroy, roll into the parking lot of the Happy Jackrabbit, he had waved him down.

Over the next fifteen minutes, they'd gathered quite a crowd around the truck. The manager of the motel, his nephew, and Leroy's cousin, Darnell, had all stopped to offer their advice. Unfortunately, they didn't seem to know much more than Colin about the inner workings of a pickup truck. Instead, all four of them preferred to review the events of the previous night, focusing most of their attention on the quantity of liquor they had consumed and the amount of money they'd lost.

Leroy turned his head and spit out a wad of tobacco juice, then went back to studying the engine.

"She always ran like a top," he said. "Drove her every day till I bought my new truck. Can't figure what could have happened."

"Maybe we should get a mechanic from the gas station," Colin suggested. "I'm afraid I don't know much about cars. Or trucks."

"Nah, me neither," Leroy said. "But I always kept this baby running." He reached into the engine compartment, then grunted. "Well, here's yer problem. Someone's been messin' with yer distributor cap."

The other men gathered around and poked their heads under the hood, adding their own comments to Leroy's diagnosis. He pointed to the offending part. "See here, it's been loosened. That's why your truck won't start."

"I did hit a bump in the parking lot when I drove it over here," Colin said. "I probably knocked it loose."

Leroy laughed, a big booming sound that carried on the brisk wind. "You city boys! Naw, that wouldn't do it. Somebody popped the hood and fixed it so you couldn't start this truck."

"Who would do something like that?" Colin asked.

Leroy straightened and wiped the grease off his hands and onto his flannel shirt. "Beats me," he said. "There are some strange folks roundabout these parts."

Colin felt as if he was standing among four of Skull Creek's strangest. "Can you fix it?"

"Already did," Leroy replied. "Just had to snap it back on. Go on, give her a try. She should start now."

Colin hopped into the truck and turned the ignition. As promised, the engine came to life. He turned the ignition back off and jumped out. "Thanks," he said. "I appreciate the help."

Leroy shrugged his bearlike shoulders. "No problem. You won her fair and square, though I can't say as I've ever seen a guy luckier at cards than you. I anted up a workin' truck and I'm honor bound to make sure that's what you got."

Colin thanked the group again and watched as they all wandered off in different directions. Then he turned back to the truck and stared at it for a long moment. A slow realization dawned in his mind. If Isabelle Channing knew how to hot-wire a car and pick a lock, she probably knew how to disable a truck.

But why?

I love you, too.

The words drifted through his mind and he closed his eyes against the harsh morning sun. Since he'd walked out on her the night before, he'd tried to put what had happened between them out of his head. And he'd managed quite nicely until now. But given a few free moments to think, it all came rushing back—the incredible need, the unfettered pleasure, the sensation of her skin beneath his palms.

He opened his eyes and looked long and hard at the truck. That's what this was about. She'd fixed the truck so they'd have to spend another night together in Skull Creek. If she delayed them long enough, they wouldn't be able to make it to Mexico before the end of the day.

So this was all about sex, he reasoned. Because it couldn't be about love. Even though she'd said the words, it was only an instinctual response to his own admission—words that had slipped out in the heat of passion. Anyone could see Isabelle hated him—or at least disliked him very intensely—outside of the bedroom. Maybe wrecking the truck was just another way to provoke him.

Colin rubbed his forehead again, his headache growing stronger with his confusion. The remnants of a hangover were muddling his brain. It was hard enough trying to figure out Isabelle with a clear head. He didn't have a chance on five hours of sleep and too much beer the night before.

He shoved the truck keys in his pocket and wandered back into the room. With a low groan, Colin flopped down on the bed and closed his eyes. He'd just begun to drift off to sleep when he heard the door open. Through slitted eyes, he watched as Isabelle tiptoed inside, closing the door quietly behind her. She placed the bag she carried on the dresser, then stared at him for a long moment, her expression unreadable.

His wife, he mused. Isabelle Channing Spencer. He had tried not to think of her in those terms, but it was getting harder all the time to maintain a safe distance. He liked being around Isabelle. She made him feel alive, as if he was living his own life, not some pale imitation of his father's existence.

He could almost imagine a future with her, how it would be to wake up with her beside him and to fall asleep with her in his arms. He'd come home from work and she'd be there, smiling, laughing. And they'd talk and share the events of their days. He could say anything to Isabelle.

Colin used to know what he wanted from a wife, but all that had changed. It had nothing at all to do with outward appearances, but with inner passions.

With Isabelle, he teetered on the edge of chaos, his emotions barely under control. But when he looked into her eyes, he knew with a certainly that was both reassuring and frightening that Isabelle belonged in his life.

He knew how he felt. So how did she feel? Did her declaration of love have any basis in reality? Did she think about a future with him? If he had at least some idea of what she truly wanted, maybe he'd know how to proceed. But with all the emotion Isabelle expended in a day, Colin still couldn't see into her heart.

He watched through half-hooded eyes as Isabelle picked up the shirt he'd discarded before his shower. At first, he thought she was going to fold it up and put it in his open suitcase. But then she pressed it to her nose and drew in a deep breath, her fingers clutching at the fabric.

She winced and groaned softly. If she was looking for the scent of his cologne, it had probably been obliterated by the smell of cigar smoke and stale beer. But that didn't matter! A woman didn't go around sniffing a man's shirt unless she had some serious feelings for him. Nor did she tamper with his distributor cap.

He rolled over on his side and pushed up on his elbow. "Did you find some breakfast?" he asked.

Isabelle jumped, then tossed his shirt on a nearby chair. "I—I didn't realize you were awake."

"I wasn't. But I am now. What's in the bag?"

"The bag?"

"On the dresser," he said. "Is that breakfast?"

She nodded. "Coffee and doughnuts."

He pushed off the bed and stood up, stretching his

arms over his head. "You know, I was just thinking we might want to stick around another day."

Isabelle blinked in surprise. "Here? Why would we want to stay here?"

She was quite a little actress when she tried, Colin mused. But if Isabellian psychology held, she would insist on doing the exact opposite of what he wanted. "I'm pretty tired. And I really don't feel like getting in that rickety old truck right now. I thought we could just stay here, curl up in bed and take a nice, long nap. How does that sound?"

"I—I think we should get on the road," Isabelle said. "I know how anxious you are to get this divorce." She cleared her throat. "You are anxious to get this divorce, aren't you?"

He combed his hair with his fingers, then shrugged. "No more anxious than you."

"All right," she said, her tone defiant. "Let's go. I'm ready."

Colin grinned as he picked up his bag and shoved the rest of his belongings into it. A few minutes later, they opened the door and walked into the bright desert sunshine. He wedged her bags behind the front seat and tossed his own into the back of the pickup. Then he strolled around to the passenger-side door and opened it.

"Your chariot awaits."

Isabelle handed him the bag with their breakfast inside, stepped up on the running board and slid onto the seat. He put the bag on her lap, shut the door, then ran around to the other side. When he joined her, she gave him a bright smile.

But when he turned the ignition and the truck roared to life, her smile gradually faded, to be replaced by a frown. "What's wrong?" he asked, his suspicions confirmed.

"Oh, nothing. The engine sounds...good."

He put the truck into reverse and twisted around to look out the back window. "Runs like a top. It should get us all the way to Mexico."

She leaned back in the seat and stared out the front window as they pulled onto the highway and headed south. "That's good," she murmured. "Because that's exactly where I want to go. Mexico."

ISABELLE WASN'T SURE when she'd fallen asleep. After a while, the scenery she'd found so beautiful during the first part of their drive took on a boring sameness. Colorless deserts with gray mountain ranges ringing the horizon. An endless strip of highway laid out in front of them. And every now and then, a small town or a cluster of trailers to break the monotony. She had closed her eyes, just to avoid the dry, dusty air swirling inside the truck. The next time she opened them, they were driving down narrow streets filled with tourists and noisy vendors selling straw hats and colorful blankets.

She sat up straight and rubbed a crick from her neck. "Are we here?"

Colin glanced over at her and smiled. "You've been sleeping a long time," he said. "You must have been tired."

"I guess I was. How are you doing?"

Colin shrugged. "I'll be happy to park this truck. The people down here drive like maniacs."

The millennium celebration in Tijuana showed no signs of slowing down. Though it was a Sunday afternoon, tourists and natives alike crowded the streets, shouting and dancing and deftly avoiding speeding cars. Like Las Vegas, the city pulsed with a party mood. The town was filled with millennium revelers, drawn across the border by the bullfights and the dog track, the shopping and the cheap tequila. The mix of American commercialism with Mexican charm gave Tijuana a slightly exotic, yet rowdy, atmosphere.

"Do you know where we're going?" Isabelle asked.

He peered out his window, then pulled the truck over to the curb in front of a small hotel. "This is it. Hotel Florencia. The guard at the border crossing suggested it."

Isabelle stared up at the hotel, a plain stucco-covered building painted in a faded shade of peach. Wrought-iron balconies surrounded the windows on the second and third floors and flowers tumbled from pots near the front door.

"I guess we're going to have to stay another night," Isabelle said.

"I doubt if we can get a divorce on a Sunday," Colin replied. He jumped out of the truck, grabbed her bags from behind the seat and circled the front bumper to open her door. Her knees wobbled slightly and he slipped his arm around her waist as he walked her to the front door of the hotel.

The plain exterior did nothing to hint at the quaint and welcoming interior. Though the Hotel Florencia was old and a bit shabby, it was meticulously clean and well tended. The desk clerk immediately rushed to help them with their luggage, then efficiently checked them in.

As the man walked them through a set of French

doors, Isabelle drew a sharp breath. The hotel was built around a lovely courtyard, brimming with exotic plants and flowers. The noise from the street seemed to fade into the distance and Isabelle looked up at a songbird perched on a palm, singing a sweet melody.

"It's beautiful," she murmured.

The desk clerk explained that the hotel served dinner for the guests between seven and nine, and a light breakfast was available in the morning. He led them up an outside stairway with an ornate wrought-iron railing to a room on the second level.

Like the rest of the hotel, their room was furnished in threadbare decor. The floor was a cool Mexican tile covered with colorful rag rugs. Isabelle set her bags down on the bed and took a peek into the plain, but serviceable, bathroom. When she turned back around, Colin was watching her from a spot near the door.

"This really is quite nice," she said.

"Along with the truck, I won a little cash last night," he said. "I thought we might as well blow the bank for our last night as a married couple."

Isabelle felt her heart twist at the realization there would be no more nights with Colin Spencer. "What about the divorce money?" she said.

He shrugged. "I'm going to go out and try to sell my watch. That should cover it."

Isabelle glanced down at her hand, then twisted the ring off her finger. She held it out to him. "Here. You should take this. We'll need some money to get home."

Colin hesitated before he took the ring from her.

He nodded. "I should probably go and take care of this now."

"I—I'll come with you," Isabelle offered.

"No, you stay here. Relax, take a bath, sleep a little more. I'll be back before dinner." He turned to leave, then glanced back over his shoulder. "Don't go out alone," he warned. "This town isn't safe for a woman alone."

Isabelle nodded. "Don't worry, I'll stay right here."

He smiled as if pleased with her uncustomary compliance. He pulled the door shut, leaving her alone in the room. Isabelle stood staring at the door for a long time, wondering at the sudden distance that had opened up between them. He seemed apprehensive and aloof and almost afraid to look at her.

She glanced down at her finger again. Odd how naked it looked without the ring. In just a few days, she'd gotten used to wearing it. It made her feel married, even if the circumstances of their union were a bit bizarre. But now that she'd taken off the diamond, Isabelle felt as if a bond between them had been irrevocably broken.

If this was what breaking up a three-day marriage was like, Isabelle knew she'd never want to go through another divorce. A hollow feeling had settled into the place where her heart was, and every time she looked at Colin, she knew that soon it would be the last time.

How would she forget him? Maybe if she threw herself back into her work or took a nice long vacation. She could always start dating someone else. Or she could give up men completely—that way she'd never have to compare a new man to Colin Spencer.

Whatever happened, Isabelle knew her future would be diminished somehow because Colin would be gone from her life.

"I don't love him," she murmured, clenching her fists at her side. "I don't. I can't." She drew in a deep breath. "I won't."

Her thoughts skipped to a time in the not-too-distant future. She'd be reading the *Tribune* over coffee one morning and she'd see the announcement of Colin's wedding. Maybe there would be a picture of him and Maggie. Or perhaps another woman would be smiling beside him, dressed in white, for Isabelle wasn't ready to believe Maggie would take him back.

Either way, he'd have himself the wife he had always wanted, a picture-perfect bride with a sweet disposition and a spotless reputation. Mrs. Spencer—whoever she was—would settle into a life that revolved around her husband. And there would be children, of course. A boy, maybe two, and a girl...lovely children with Colin's smile and his eyes.

Isabelle moaned softly and pressed the heels of her hands to her temples. This was what made divorce so difficult! All the futile hopes and unreconciled regrets. She would never have a future with Colin, she'd never walk down a flower-strewn aisle. And there wouldn't be any children.

"I never wanted to get married in the first place," Isabelle said, throwing herself on the bed. She pulled a pillow over her eyes and tried to clear her mind of every thought involving him. But when she pushed him aside, she became aware of how sticky her skin was, how tangled her hair had become. With a frustrated groan, she got up from the bed and began to strip her clothes off. Then, barefoot, she padded into the bathroom and ran a hot bath.

The water felt wonderful on her dry, dusty skin. Isabelle held her breath, then submerged, getting her hair completely wet. As she lay back in the warm water, resting her head on the edge of the tub, she closed her eyes. Images of Colin danced across her brain. The harder she tried to put him out of her head, the more he invaded her thoughts.

The only way to get him completely out of her mind was to fall into a deep and dreamless sleep. Isabelle closed her eyes and tried to slow her breathing, tried to let go of all the doubts, the warm water relaxing her. There would come a day when she'd barely remember him…the way he touched her…the way his mouth felt when he kissed her…

The next time she opened her eyes, the bathroom was nearly dark, her fingers had turned pruney and the bathwater was cold. With a soft cry, she scrambled out of the tub and snatched a towel. Her teeth chattered as she hurried to the bed and dumped out the bags of clothes. She chose the only dress she hadn't worn and pulled it over her body, not bothering with underwear.

Her hair had dried into a wavy mass that still had traces of road dust in it. She grabbed a brush and pulled her hair back into a sleek knot, fastening it with the bobby pins left over from New Year's Eve. When she felt presentable, she sat down on the edge of the bed and waited for Colin to return.

He'd been gone nearly two hours. Anxious, she pushed up from the bed and went over to the windows, throwing them open. Then she went to the door on the opposite side of the room and opened it.

The soft night breeze slipped through the room but did nothing to alleviate her nerves.

She began to pace, and when that wasn't enough, Isabelle walked out onto the balcony and stared down into the courtyard. Colorful lights had been strung through the trees, softly illuminating the guests below. A guitarist wandered among the tables, singing a sweet Spanish tune. But the music did nothing to relax her. As the minutes passed, her worries increased and Isabelle imagined an endless string of troubling events. Colin had been lost...or hurt...or kidnapped or maybe even—she swallowed hard—killed.

By the time he came bounding up the steps a half-hour later, Isabelle had formulated a detailed story involving drug runners and pawnshop brokers and a corrupt police department. He smiled when he saw her, but the stormy look on her face caused his good mood to immediately fade. "Where were you?" she demanded, stalking up to him. "You've been gone nearly three hours. I was worried."

His grin returned. "You were worried? About me?" He chuckled. "Poetic justice. Now you know how I feel most of the time."

"I asked you a question," Isabelle said, keenly aware they'd reversed roles, yet unwilling to concede the point.

"I drove back across the border," he explained. "When I tried to pawn the watch here, they wanted to give me pesos. So I drove back up to San Ysidro and found a pawnshop there." He reached into his pocket and withdrew an envelope filled with cash, took out a few bills and handed her the rest.

"What's this?" she asked.

"Money," he said.

"I don't want your money," Isabelle replied, turning away from him and walking back into the room.

He followed hard on her heels. "Don't be so stubborn. Think of it as community property. We purchased these things while we were married. They're half yours. Besides, you'll need money to get home."

"I'm perfectly capable of taking care of myself," she said. Isabelle bristled at the thought of taking a single cent from Colin. But he was right. With his poker winnings, they had about two hundred dollars to pay for their trip home, not nearly enough to get her back to Chicago. And then she had to deal with the stolen rental car which she'd put on *her* credit card.

"Damn it, Isabelle, just take the money. You don't have to use it to go to Chicago. Take a vacation, get away for a while, go back to Vegas and gamble it away. I don't care."

With a soft curse, she snatched the envelope from his fingers and tossed it on the bed. "Of course, you don't care."

He sighed, then stepped toward her. "That's not what I meant." Colin reached down and tipped her chin up with his finger. "I just want you to be happy, that's all. This has been difficult for both of us. If you need some time before you go back to Chicago, I think you should take it."

She turned away, refusing to meet his gaze. Time was not going to help. Time would only make her loneliness more acute, her memories more intolerable. She heard him sigh again as he stepped away and grabbed his bag from where he'd placed it at the foot of the bed. An emptiness settled into her heart.

Why couldn't they just pick up where they'd left off last night, passion flaring between them, need overwhelming common sense? Isabelle wanted to take his hand and draw him over to the bed, to slip into his embrace and lose herself in the feel of her body against his. Making love with Colin Spencer had been only a bothersome fantasy. But now that they were so close to divorce, to walking away from each other for good, she wanted to experience him just once, wild and uninhibited and aching with desire.

Isabelle swallowed hard, trying to work up the courage to make the first move. "Where are you going?" she murmured.

"I got a room right next door. I thought it might be better if you had some time to yourself. After all, tomorrow at this time, we'll be divorced. We'll have to get used to single life again." The last was said with a healthy dose of sarcasm, but Isabelle didn't find any humor in his words, just painful disappointment.

"Maybe that would be best," she murmured. She stood silently, watching him, waiting for him to say more.

With a rueful smile, he crossed the room and brushed a quick kiss across her cheek. "Good night, Isabelle. Sleep well."

She risked a glance up at him, seeing nothing in his eyes but indifference. "Good night."

When the door shut behind him, she slowly lowered herself to the bed, sitting on the edge with her hands folded on her lap. Silence settled in around her and she drew a deep breath, then let it out slowly. Maybe Colin was right. They'd have to get used to going back to their old lives…their separate lives. It was only logical.

Isabelle pressed her hand to her heart, feeling an ache deep within. Her head told her this was the right thing to do, that if she tried hard enough, she could put Colin in the past.

Now, if only she could convince her heart.

"AN OVERNIGHT DIVORCE? I'm afraid that's not possible, Señor Spencer."

Isabelle slowly sat back in her chair, trying hard to ignore the unbidden flood of relief that raced through her. She let out her tightly held breath, then drew another. Could this be true? She had just assumed once they got to Tijuana, everything would proceed without a hitch and her short-lived marriage would become just another statistic.

They had found hundreds of divorce lawyers in the phone book, all offering quick and painless procedures. But Colin had relied on the desk clerk at their hotel for a recommendation. Coincidentally, the man's cousin ran a practice a few blocks away. The clerk had called and set up an appointment for later that morning and they'd arrived at the tiny storefront office right on time.

Isabelle had slept fitfully the night before, the sounds of Tijuana intruding on her dreams. She wondered how many other couples had married in haste on the eve of the millennium and repented a few days later, how many of those they passed on the street were headed in the same direction.

As she lay in bed earlier that morning, her thoughts were constantly focused on the room next door. She had pictured Colin lying in bed, stripped of his clothes, his naked body twisted in the sheets. The urge to go to him, to pick up where they had left off the previous night in Skull Creek, was nearly overwhelming. Isabelle knew if they made love there would be no denying the bond they had formed.

She had crawled out of bed at least four or five times and walked to the door, determined to confront him, to wrap her arms around his neck and lose herself in his kisses, in his touch. He wouldn't be able to resist her and he'd carry her to the bed and tug at her clothes until there was nothing but skin between them. She would tease him and test him, until he could no longer deny himself, and his passions would drive him over the edge.

A soft sigh slipped from her throat, the sound drawing her back to the present.

"Not possible?" Colin said. He leaned forward and placed his hands on Mr. Vasquez's desk. "I don't understand. If it's the money, I can—"

The lawyer held up his hand and shook his head. "It is not the money, *señor*. It is the law. Although there is no residency requirement, here in Mexico it takes four months to get a divorce."

"Four months?" Colin groaned and flopped back in his chair. "We could have stayed in Las Vegas and gotten a divorce in six weeks!"

Mr. Vasquez nodded. "Yes, that is true. Unfortunately, it is too easy to get married in Las Vegas, but not so easy to get divorced if you do not live there. Now, if you are interested in marrying again, you will have to check the laws in the States. These I don't know well."

"I'm not interested in marrying again," Isabelle piped up with a tight smile. "Although, I can't say the same for my husband. He has a fiancée, you know. He's very anxious to get back to her."

Colin turned to Isabelle and sent her a disapproving glare. "I don't think Mr. Vasquez needs to know all the details, *darling*."

Luis Vasquez shook his head. "Actually, Señor Spencer, when you get your divorce, you will have to state a reason."

"Reason?" Colin asked, his attention snapping back to the lawyer. "We don't want to be married anymore. Isn't that reason enough?"

"Then you don't get along? This is a case of irreconcilable differences?"

"That's an understatement," Isabelle muttered. "He's overbearing and opinionated and dictatorial. He never lets me do what I want. He's always trying to boss me around."

"And she's stubborn and disobedient and impertinent," Colin countered. "And she has no respect for the institution of marriage."

"You're the one who has no respect," Isabelle accused, jumping to her feet, her fists braced on her hips.

Colin stood and faced her, his temper piqued. "And what is that supposed to mean?"

She poked a finger into his chest, punctuating her words with a painful jab. "You asked me to marry you and I did. Now, just a few days later, you want a divorce."

"I was drunk when I proposed. And I didn't see you putting up a fuss when I suggested divorce. You're just as anxious to get this over with as I am."

"Well, maybe I'm not!" Isabelle said, crossing her

arms over her chest and tipping her chin up defiantly. "Maybe I don't want a divorce!"

Clearly stunned, Colin stared at her for a long moment. Isabelle shifted on her feet, then fixed her gaze on her toes. She hadn't meant to say that. Even though it was exactly what she felt, she wasn't supposed to say it out loud. Her true feelings for Colin were not at issue here. This divorce was about *his* feelings—or lack thereof.

Mr. Vasquez cleared his throat. "I am afraid if either party contests the divorce, there will be problems. You will have to spend much more time in the courts." He reached for some papers. "Now, would you like to proceed?"

Colin reached out and took Isabelle's hand, but she snatched it away as if she'd been burned. "Do you mean it?" he murmured. "You don't want a divorce?"

The truth was, the more time she spent as Colin Spencer's wife, the more she was beginning to believe marriage to him wasn't such a bad thing. Even their worst moments together were full of fire and passion. She loved fighting with him almost as much as she loved kissing him. She'd never experienced such intense emotions for a man. And deep in her heart, she doubted she'd ever feel this way again.

Isabelle drew a shaky breath and fought back the tears that threatened to spill over the corners of her eyes. "I—I meant that I didn't want a divorce *this* way."

"Here in Mexico?"

She shook her head.

"Isabelle, if you want some kind of settlement, we can—"

"No!" she cried, her eyes wide, fury welling up inside her and banishing the tears. "Is that what you think? I'm holding out for money?" Colin held up his hand to calm her temper, but she slapped it aside. "How dare you! I've never even mentioned money. And if you offered me a million dollars, I'd throw it back in your face."

"A million dollars?" Mr. Vasquez asked, sitting up straighter. "You want *more* than a million dollars? Oh, this will take much longer than four months."

"I don't want a single penny of his money," Isabelle said, her jaw tight, her emotions in check.

Colin reached out and grasped her shoulders, forcing her to look into his eyes. When she met his gaze, she expected anger and frustration. But as she looked up at him, there was something entirely unexpected there. She saw a sliver of regret. And a glimmer of hope. And what she wanted to believe was real affection.

"Then what did you mean?" he asked softly.

This was her opportunity. It was now or never. If she thought they had a chance to make this marriage work, she had to speak now or forever hold her peace. Isabelle drew a deep breath, ready to pour out her heart. But as the words formed in her mind, she realized how utterly ridiculous, how desperate and pathetic they sounded.

What she saw in his eyes wasn't love. If he truly loved her, why was he pressing for this divorce? Why had he spent every moment over the past two days thinking of nothing but getting to Mexico and putting a quick end to their marriage? She was seeing what she wanted to see, what her fantasies had conjured in her mind, not what reality offered.

Besides, she couldn't remain married to Colin Spencer. He wanted a wife who fit into the straitlaced Spencer mold. A proper, obsequious little doormat who could charm his business associates and keep a tidy house, an automaton in an apron. Isabelle groaned inwardly. Strangely enough, she was tempted to try, to turn herself into exactly the kind of woman who would fit into Colin's world. She'd grown up in that world of privilege and social ritual, so it wouldn't be such a difficult thing, would it? If she worked at it, she could become her mother.

"Isabelle?"

She glanced up, then swallowed her silly hopes. "I—I meant that I didn't want to get a divorce with all this fighting and acrimony. That's all." Isabelle turned and picked up her sweater from where she'd laid it over the arm of her chair. Then she looked at Mr. Vasquez. "I want the divorce. Really, I do," she said.

Mr. Vasquez gave her a sympathetic look. "May I make a suggestion, Señora Spencer?"

"Please do," she said.

"You both live in Chicago, no?"

"Yes," Isabelle replied.

"If you want a quick divorce, or even an annulment, you can obtain one right there. It is possible for you to be divorced in just twenty-four hours if the procedure is uncontested. I know this because my cousin, Roberto, lives in Chicago and he got a very speedy divorce."

Colin gasped, the sound like a knife to her heart. This was what he wanted all along, but in order to end their marriage, he'd have to take her back to Chicago as his bride. In the grand scheme of things, that seemed like a minor annoyance. "We can be divorced overnight in Chicago?"

"See?" Isabelle said. "I told you you should have called your lawyer. We could have saved ourselves all this time and trouble." With that, she spun on her heel and headed toward the door.

Colin caught up to her in a few long steps and grabbed her arm. "Isabelle, wait."

She drew a ragged breath, pushed back her tears and faced him with an indifferent smile. "Don't worry," she said. "We'll go home, you'll get your divorce and we'll both live happily ever after."

"That's not what I—"

"It's exactly what you want. Our marriage was a mistake, a lapse in judgment, that's all. And what's another day or two? Just a little longer to wait before you can go back to Maggie, free and clear."

"Isabelle, I—"

She reached up and pressed her fingers to his lips. But the mere act of touching him sent a frisson of desire racing through her body, warming her blood until she felt weak and confused. "There's nothing more to say. Why don't you go back to the hotel and call your lawyer. I'm going to take a walk. I need some fresh air." He grasped her hand and, for a brief moment, she thought he might press his lips to her fingertips. Hesitantly, she drew away.

"I don't think you should be out alone on the streets. If you want to walk, I'll come with you."

Isabelle shook her head and smiled ruefully. He'd never change, not in a million years. Still, Isabelle was going to miss his protectiveness, that sweet streak of chauvinism that Colin refused to abandon.

"You're going to have to stop thinking of me as your wife," she said.

His expression softened and he bit at his lower lip, a slight frown creasing his forehead. Then he nodded. "I know." Colin shoved his hands in his pants' pockets. "I know. Go ahead. Take your walk. I'll see you back at the hotel."

Isabelle turned and headed toward the door, each step reminding her that it wouldn't be long before she walked away from Colin for good. What would the moment be like, their final goodbye? Would she be able to put him out of her mind or would her future be plagued by memories of what they'd shared and thoughts of what might have been?

She reached for the doorknob with trembling fingers, tempted to glance back. Instead, she hardened her heart and pushed back her emotions. What was done, was done. She and Colin had been married and now they'd be divorced. They'd both go on with their lives as if nothing had happened.

And when she looked back at how she'd spent the eve of the millennium, she'd smile and laugh and tell everyone of the silly trick she'd played trying to save her best friend from a bad marriage.

8

COLIN FOUND HER sitting at a table in the courtyard of the hotel. Lush foliage and heavily scented flowers filled the air with a sweet smell. A trio of guitarists stood beneath an arched colonnade, strumming a soft Spanish tune, the notes drifting into the night.

She'd been shopping and had discarded the clothes he'd bought her in favor of a pretty peasant blouse that revealed the soft curves of her shoulders and a colorful striped skirt that brushed the cobblestone courtyard. Her feet were bare and she'd tucked a flower behind her ear. She looked exotic, sultry, her dark hair falling over her back in thick waves.

As he stood in the shadows of a bougainvillea, Colin drank in the sight of her like a man dying of thirst. His gaze skimmed her features, committing each detail to memory. There would come a time in the future when he'd want to recall the exact shape of her nose, the way her lips turned up when she smiled, the delicate length of her fingers.

They'd only been apart for an afternoon, but it felt like days. After he had called his lawyer's office in Chicago, he'd knocked on her door, but she hadn't answered. The desk clerk informed him Mrs. Spencer had gone out and he spent the rest of the afternoon walking the streets, hoping he'd find her, wondering where she might be, and knowing he shouldn't care.

Tomorrow morning, they would return home. His attorney had arranged for the paperwork to be drawn up for an uncontested divorce. They would sign on the dotted line and their divorce would be set in motion. Of course, one of them was required to appear in court before the divorce was final, but his attorney had assured him he could arrange for Colin to complete this step in a prompt and discreet manner.

Everything they'd shared in the last few days would be erased, put in the past. Colin tried to imagine a time when Isabelle would fade from his memory, but he couldn't. She would follow him around for the rest of his life as a reminder of what might have been...what could still be. And he knew with certainty that he would never be able to look into a woman's eyes without seeing her.

Colin tipped his head back and inhaled the perfumed night air. He wanted to believe Isabelle had fallen in love with him, but nothing he saw in her behavior, nothing in her words, proved that notion. For a brief instant at Vasquez's office, he thought there might be a chance. When she had declared she didn't want the divorce, his heart had stopped and his hopes had soared. But once again, Isabelle had retreated behind an impenetrable wall of indifference.

"Wishful thinking," he murmured.

If he really wanted to know how she felt, why not just come right out and admit his own feelings? He was in love with his wife, it was as simple as that. Though he'd fought against any emotional attachment, Isabelle Channing made that nearly impossible. She was beautiful and exciting and captivating and he had lost his heart somewhere on the highway between Vegas and Tijuana.

But when he imagined professing his love to her, the picture never seemed to come out right. He saw Isabelle laughing at the ridiculous admission or staring at him in complete disbelief or chiding him for silly sentimentality. What he didn't see was Isabelle falling into his arms and repeating those words herself. The last man in the world Isabelle Channing would choose to love was Colin Spencer.

He shook his head. It was time to forget any fantasies of a happy marriage. From this night on, he had to think of himself as a single man with no claims on Isabelle's heart or her body. In just a day or two, they'd no longer be husband and wife. He *would* forget Isabelle Channing. He had no choice.

Colin stepped out of the shadows and headed toward her table. When he got there, she glanced up at him and his breath caught in his throat. The soft light of a candle, glowing in the middle of the table, cast her face in gold. A tentative smile touched her lips and he fought the temptation to lean over and brush his mouth against hers.

"Hi," she said, the word slipping from her throat like a soft sigh. "You're back."

Colin pulled out the chair across from her and sat down. "I've arranged for our flight back to Chicago," he said. "And my attorney will meet with us tomorrow evening to sign the papers."

She picked up her glass and took a slow sip of her drink, then carefully set it back down again. "So fast. So painless. It's almost like we were never married at all."

Colin nodded. He'd never seen Isabelle like this,

calm and remote. He expected anger or forced gaiety, not complete apathy. He fought an urge to reach out and shake her, to goad her into an argument in the hopes her feelings would spill out along with her temper. But she seemed so fragile and vulnerable, as if one wrong word would cause her to shatter into a million pieces.

"Isabelle, I think it might be best if we talk—"

"Now is not the time for recriminations," she said, forcing a smile. "This is our last night as a married couple. We should celebrate." She motioned to the waiter and ordered two fresh margaritas.

"I know I shouldn't let you drink," she teased, her levity as artificial as her smile. "But I promise I won't drag you off to a wedding chapel and marry you all over again. We won't be repeating this little disaster."

"It wasn't such a disaster," Colin said. "In fact, I had a lot of fun."

She refused to meet his gaze, her eyes lowered to stare at the flickering flame of the candle. When the drinks arrived, she almost looked relieved at finding something to occupy her attention. She picked up her glass and held it out toward him. "A toast," she said. "To strange beginnings and happy endings."

He raised his glass. "To our marriage."

She hesitated before she touched her glass to his, then took a sip of her drink. "So, what are your plans for after the divorce?" she asked. "I suppose you're anxious to set things right with Maggie."

Colin hadn't really thought about it until that very moment. But his plan didn't take much consideration. "I do have to talk to her," he said.

"What are you going to tell her?" Isabelle asked, her voice catching slightly.

"That I can't marry her."

Isabelle coughed, then covered her mouth with her fingers. Her eyes watered and she snatched up her napkin. Colin quickly stood and placed his palm on her back. As soon as he touched her, he knew he'd made a mistake. Her bare skin was like silk beneath his fingers and her fragrant hair brushed the back of his hand. "Are you all right?" he asked, patting her back.

She waved him away, nodding. "I just swallowed wrong."

When she had finally stopped coughing, he resumed his place across from her and studied her openly. Color bloomed in her cheeks and her eyes were dewy with moisture. A tear slipped from the corner of her eye and Colin reached out and caught it with his thumb, his palm lingering on her cheek.

"You're sure you're all right?" he asked. Her nonchalant attitude had crumbled in front of his eyes and he watched as conflicting emotions warred for control of her pretty face.

"You—you aren't going to marry Maggie?" she asked. "When did you decide that?"

Her words were soft and faltering and filled with disbelief. Surely she'd realized by now he could never marry Maggie Kelley. A man didn't just fall into bed with his fiancée's best friend and then expect to go on with the wedding plans. He'd nearly made love with Isabelle the night before. And the night before that, he *had* made love with her, though he couldn't remember all the details.

"You were right," he said.

"I was?"

"That night in the elevator. I was marrying her for all the wrong reasons. I wasn't being honest with myself and I certainly wasn't being fair to her. You were right."

A tremulous smile played across her mouth and she reached out for the menu the waiter had placed on the table. "Maybe we should get something to eat. I'm famished."

They passed the next hour chatting about inconsequential subjects, never venturing into territory too intimate. They didn't talk of the past or the future. Instead, they seized upon subjects completely benign and uncontroversial—the weather, the sights in Tijuana, the names of the tunes the guitarists played.

Through it all, Isabelle remained steadfastly subdued. Usually she was quick to offer an opinion or initiate an argument, but tonight she was demure and complaisant. He should have found their dinner enjoyable, but Colin felt as if he were dining with a complete stranger. As the night went on, she grew more distant, more inaccessible. The fire in her was slowly dying and he didn't know how to stop it.

When the waiter brought the check, Colin signed for the dinner, then pushed back from the table. He held out his hand to Isabelle as he stood. "Why don't we take a walk?" he suggested. "We should enjoy our time in Mexico. We'll be going back to chilly weather in Chicago too soon."

Isabelle carefully folded her napkin and placed it on the table. "I'm really not in the mood for a walk," she said. "I think I just want to go to my room. I'm tired and that last margarita gave me a headache."

Colin tucked her hand in the crook of his elbow

and led her across the courtyard. They climbed the outside stairway to the second level of the hotel, then walked along the balcony, staring down at the court-yard. When they reached the door of Isabelle's room, Colin paused, and took her hands in his.

"I want to thank you," he murmured. "I'm not sure what might have happened if I hadn't gotten into that elevator with you."

"You might have had a happy marriage, instead of—" She swallowed hard. "Instead of this mess."

"It wasn't such mess," he said. "And I know now Maggie isn't the kind of woman I want to marry."

She glanced away, unwilling to look into his eyes, feigning interest in a flowering vine hanging over the ornate railing of the balcony. "Wha-what kind of woman do you want to marry?"

"I don't know. Someone exciting…full of life. Someone who will make every day an adventure. A woman I can look at for hours and still find something new in her face."

A woman just like you, Colin wanted to say. As the words drifted through his mind, he knew they weren't exactly right. He didn't want a woman *just* like Isabelle. He wanted Isabelle.

"I should go," she said. "We have a busy day ahead of us tomorrow."

He knew she was making excuses, that she was as uncertain of what lay ahead as he was. When they'd set off for Tijuana a few days ago, the only thing Colin was interested in was ending his marriage.

Now, as he stood here with Isabelle, the soft night breeze blowing in her hair, the scent of her perfume teasing at his nose, he wanted time to stop. He needed just a few more hours with her to convince himself he could make it work, that they could have a future together.

But when she turned and opened the door of her room and walked inside, he couldn't bring himself to stop her. All he could think about was the myriad reasons why she couldn't possibly love him. And all the reasons why he knew he loved her.

ISABELLE LEANED BACK against the door and closed her eyes, trying to still the furious pounding of her heart. She took a deep breath and then another until her mind began to clear.

Only one thought filled her brain, one unbelievable, inconceivable thought. Colin Spencer wasn't going to marry Maggie Kelley! She should have felt some smug sense of satisfaction. After all, that's why she'd spirited him off to Las Vegas in the first place—to keep him from ruining her best friend's life.

But instead of satisfaction, she was filled with hope. If Colin wasn't going to marry Maggie, there was a chance he might love her. And since Maggie didn't love him... Her mind jumped back to the previous night, to the words she and Colin had exchanged. How could they be true? They barely knew each other. They'd spent a weekend together and yet she felt as if she'd known Colin her entire life.

Isabelle had always believed in love at first sight, the kind of love that could knock a girl over and steal her senses, love that sprang to life in a matter of minutes and lasted forever. She'd always believed but she never thought it would happen to her.

Could she be meant to spend her life with Colin Spencer? She'd fallen for exactly the kind of man her mother wanted her to marry—stable, dependable, wealthy. And yet none of that mattered. Colin was kind and generous and passionate. His mere touch made her heart skip and her knees go weak.

She closed her eyes and tried to imagine them together, tried to fabricate a picture of their life in Chicago. As the image came into focus, she gradually realized she couldn't place herself in the picture. She'd suffocate under the weight of his family's expectations. Dress this way, act that way, speak sweetly and don't say anything too controversial. Keep your opinions to yourself and always agree with your husband.

There would be endless rounds of parties, social obligations that would bore her to tears. She'd be forced to quit her job, to turn her life into something she could barely tolerate. In the end, she'd be miserable, like a pretty bird trapped in a cage, waiting for just one chance to fly away.

"And we'd end up right back here," Isabelle murmured, rubbing her temples with her fingers. "Waiting to end a marriage that should have never happened in the first place."

If she couldn't have a future with him, she decided, she'd have one more night. They were still married. He was no longer engaged to Maggie. So there was nothing standing between them now. She could walk out of this room, knock on his door and let passion run its course.

Isabelle hurried into the bathroom and ran a brush through her hair, then grabbed the perfume Colin had bought her and dabbed a bit on her neck and wrists. Staring at her reflection in the mirror, she pulled her peasant blouse down until it revealed a tiny bit of cleavage.

"I couldn't sleep," she practiced, speaking to her reflection in the mirror. Isabelle frowned. "No, that won't work. I just told him I was tired." She ran her fingers through her hair. "I should be honest." She cleared her throat. "Let's have sex." She groaned. "Too aggressive."

She stepped out of the bathroom and sat down at the end of the bed, smoothing her skirt nervously. "Take a deep breath," she murmured. "You've seduced men before. This is no different...except maybe for the fact you're madly in love with him." Suddenly, the room seemed to close in on her. She pushed up from the bed and crossed to the door. Isabelle threw it open and stepped outside, drawing a deep breath of the sweet night air filtering up from the courtyard.

"Couldn't sleep?"

She turned to find Colin standing outside his own door. His elbows were braced on the wrought-iron railing and he stared down at the candlelit tables below. "The room was a little stuffy," she said. "I'll just leave you to—"

"No," he said. "Stay."

"A-all right." She looked down and watched as a happy couple kissed over glasses of wine, the trio of guitarists serenading them with a love song. She could have those same romantic feelings, at least for one more night. Isabelle gathered up her courage. "I was just thinking—"

"So was I," he interrupted. "I was thinking about that night. In Las Vegas. Our wedding night. Or maybe it was our wedding morning."

"What about it?"

"I don't remember much about it," he said.

"That's strange since I remember the rest of the night. I even remember the wedding cere-mony...vaguely."

"I—I better go in," she said, unable to maintain her composure. She should tell him the truth! They'd never consummated their marriage and he had a right to know that. But Isabelle couldn't admit she'd deceived him. The feelings he still had for her were so fragile, an admission like that could destroy them completely. She hurried back into the room but he only followed her.

"Don't you think it's strange?" he asked.

"You had too much champagne," she said. "Now, I'm really tired and I—"

"Tell me about it," Colin said.

Isabelle gasped. "What?"

"Tell me. A guy only has one wedding night and I'd like to know what happened." He stepped nearer. "Did I kiss you?"

"Of—of course you kissed me," Isabelle lied. "A lot. I mean, many times."

"And the first time?"

"We were standing next to the bed," she said, making up the story as she went along.

He snagged her waist and drew her toward the bed. She wanted to pull away, but his arms felt good around her body.

"Here?" he asked. "Or on the other side."

She risked a glance up at him. "Right here."

"Then what happened?"

Isabelle sighed. "Is this really so important? We're getting a divorce. I'd think you'd want to forget our wedding night."

"I can't forget what I don't remember," he said with a shrug. "Was I good?"

She nodded, a warm flush stealing up her cheeks. "You were…very good. Spectacular." There! Maybe that would end the conversation and he'd leave. That's probably what he was fishing for anyway, a confirmation he'd done his husbandly duty in an outstanding fashion.

"And how did it start? I mean, what did I do first?"

Isabelle groaned inwardly. There had to be a way to end this ridiculous inquisition. "First, you kissed me."

"Where?"

"Next to the bed. I already told you that."

"No, I mean, where? On the mouth?" He brushed a fleeting kiss on her lips. "Or on the neck?" He found the sensitive skin beneath her ear and pressed his hot mouth against her skin. "Or maybe it was your shoulder?" His fingers slid along her collar-bone, hooking beneath her blouse and sweeping it off her shoulder until his lips found the perfect spot.

Isabelle swallowed hard. This was not going well. The more she talked, the more he questioned her. "I—I really can't recall, exactly," she said. Not that she was trying! The only thing she could think about was the way his lips felt on her skin right now.

"But it felt good?"

She drew a ragged breath. "Really good."

His tongue traced a line from her collarbone to her jaw. "Like this?"

"Umm," she replied, a tremor catching her voice. "Just like that."

With a low moan, he pulled her closer and covered

her mouth with his. "Tell me more, Isabelle," he murmured, his lips soft on hers. "Tell me what you want."

She wanted him to stop touching her, to stop making her head spin and her heart pound. But she couldn't say that. Instead, Isabelle said the only words that rang true. "I—I want you to make love with me." She tipped her head back and closed her eyes. "I want you to be my husband, for just one more night."

He cupped her face in his hands, forcing her to meet his gaze. "And I want you to be my wife," he said. Then he kissed her again, this time with such exquisite purity and startling tenderness he touched the depths of her soul and the hidden corners of her heart.

She was exhilarated and frightened at the same time. This man—her husband—held such power over her. Her life had become so tangled in his she wasn't sure where her feelings began and ended. She couldn't control her heart any more than she could control her desire for him—and she didn't want to.

Isabelle drew back, reached for the buttons of his shirt and slowly worked them open, one by one. When she had finished, she slipped her hands beneath the fabric and smoothed her palms over his chest. Muscle rippled beneath her fingers and she pressed her mouth to the soft dusting of hair at the base of his neck.

"What happened next?" he asked, nuzzling his face in her hair.

"Next?"

"That night," Colin said. "What happened after I kissed you by the bed?"

"I—I can't remember," Isabelle replied.

He grabbed the cuffs of his shirt and tugged it off, revealing broad shoulders and a narrow waist. Isabelle couldn't seem to take her eyes off his body, so drawn by the masculine perfection of it. "Did I undress you, or did you undress me?"

She blinked, then glanced up at him. "I—I don't—"

He slipped his fingers beneath the gathered neckline of her peasant blouse and lowered it along her upper arms an inch and then one more. "I bet we worked on it together. Kind of like this." His gaze fixed on the spot where his fingers rested. "One piece of clothing at a time, first you and then me."

Slowly, the blouse slipped down until the tops of her breasts were bare. Colin leaned over and kissed her, exploring every inch of exposed skin with his tongue. And when he ran out of new territory, his fingers tugged a little farther until he took her nipple into his mouth and gently sucked.

Isabelle moaned, exquisite sensations radiating from the spot where his mouth touched her and racing to her very core. Desire welled up inside her, hot and reckless, anxious for release. As his mouth drifted lower still, she reached down and grasped the hem of her blouse, then yanked it over her head in one quick motion.

He'd pulled away and now stared down at her body, naked from the waist up. "I don't remember this," he said. "I don't remember you being so incredibly beautiful." Tenderly, almost reverently, he touched her breast, cupping the warm flesh in his palm and rubbing his thumb over the hardened nipple.

Isabelle tried to focus her thoughts, to remember every sensation so she might recall it later. No man had ever made her feel so cherished, so alluring, so...loved. Colin had watched over her and protected her the past few days. And now, as he touched her so intimately, she had to believe he loved her, at least a little.

Hesitantly, she reached for his belt and began to work the buckle open. But when her hands brushed against his erection, so hot and hard beneath the fabric of his pants, he froze, sucking in a sharp breath. "I should have remembered that," he said with a rueful smile. "The way your touch almost takes me over the edge."

"I—I'm sorry," Isabelle said.

He took her hands and drew them back. "There's nothing to be sorry about. Not anymore."

With that, he pulled her body against his and kissed her, his tongue delving deep into her mouth, demanding, enticing, overwhelming her with passion. Their lips still melded, they tore frantically at each other's clothes, pausing only for a fleeting caress here and there.

When they finally tossed aside the last barriers between them, skin instantly met skin, warm and smooth. Her breasts pressed against his chest and his shaft branded her belly. This was how it was supposed to be between a husband and wife, such raw intimacy with nothing held back. Her limbs went boneless, and just when she thought she might lose the ability to stand, he picked her up and carried her to the bed.

Gently, he laid her down and then bent over her, his mouth teasing at the curve of her neck. He drew back for a moment and grabbed something from the back pocket of his pants. He held out the foil package and Isabelle stared at it for a long time. "Did you know this was going to happen?" she asked.

He smiled and kissed her again. "I hoped." He pressed his lips against her throat. "And now what? Tell me how it was."

Isabelle drew a ragged breath. "It was like this," she said, opening the condom. With trembling fingers, she sheathed his hard arousal, then guided him to her, anticipating the feel of him slipping inside her.

Patiently, deliciously, he probed her entrance, teasing her with the promise of what they might share, heightening her own desire. Isabelle twisted beneath him, stroking him until he murmured a soft plea in her ear. He grabbed her wrists and cuffed her hands over her head. And then, he lowered his weight onto her hips and slipped inside her, smooth as silk and hard as steel, his gaze locked with hers.

Isabelle's pulse pounded and her breath froze in her throat as he drove toward her core. She had looked into his eyes so many times before, only to see anger and frustration, even desire. But now, as he buried himself deep within her and slowly began to move, she saw something more in his gaze. She saw love.

With a soft sigh, Isabelle arched against him and gave herself over to the feel of his body inside hers. There were no more questions, no demands, just the crystal-clear knowledge that they belonged together. And the words they'd spoken in such haste a few nights before had not been a mistake. Isabelle loved

Colin Spencer. And she knew in her heart he loved her.

They made love again and again, in so many different ways, until they were both pleasantly exhausted, their hunger for each other sated. Isabelle lay wrapped in his arms, her body nestled into the curve of his, his chest pressed against her back and his legs tangled with hers.

"So that's the way it was," he murmured, his breath tickling the nape of her neck.

She smiled. "No. This time was different," she said.

He kissed her neck, then rested his chin on her shoulder. "You're right. This time felt like the first time. The very first time. Why do you think that was?"

Colin didn't have to say any more. He knew. Somehow he'd figured out she'd lied about their first night together. Why should she be surprised? He remembered almost everything else, including their wedding ceremony. After what they'd shared tonight, was it any wonder he realized there was nothing to remember about their wedding night?

Isabelle grabbed his palm and kissed the tips of his fingers. "The very first time," she repeated.

She stared at his hand and kissed each fingertip, then traced the lines crisscrossing his palm. What would happen now, now that they'd finally come together? What was the next hurdle they'd have to overcome—his family, Maggie, her job? Her mind became a jumble of doubts about the future, but all that came to an abrupt halt when her eyes came to rest on a familiar sight.

"The mark of the millennium," she murmured.

"What?" Colin asked.

Isabelle blinked, hoping her exhaustion was affecting her vision. But when she looked again, it was there, as clear as day, just at the base of his thumb. "This mark. The lines in your palm form a star. It's the mark of the millennium."

He held his palm out in front of her. "Oh, right. The Gypsy lady at the party told me about that. Some story about destiny and…I don't know. I didn't pay much attention."

Isabelle's heart twisted until she was sure it had stopped beating and she was about to die. This had all been a mistake, the passion, the emotion. She wasn't supposed to love him and he couldn't love her! He and Maggie both had the mark. And *she* had been the one to rip them apart!

She fought the urge to tear herself away from him, to leave the bed they'd shared and take herself somewhere where she might sort this all out. But Colin hugged her closer to his body and sighed softly. There was no escape. Not now. As she listened to his breathing grow slow and even, Isabelle's mind raced.

Colin Spencer could never love her. And though he was here with her now, he was supposed to spend the rest of his life with Maggie Kelley!

HE WOKE UP SLOWLY, reluctantly, his body still exhausted, his muscles completely relaxed. Colin opened his eyes to the morning light, then smiled. He wasn't sure how much sleep he'd had, but it wasn't more than four or five hours. That was enough. He didn't want to waste another minute without Isabelle in his arms.

He reached over for her but her side of the bed was cold and empty. Colin pushed up on his elbow and looked around the room through a sleepy gaze. The room was silent and the bathroom door ajar. He rubbed his eyes, then squinted at the bedside clock. "Seven-thirty," he murmured. Three hours' sleep.

A slow realization hit him and he sat up and shook his head. Had he dreamed it all? Colin scanned the room, but there was no sign Isabelle had been there the night before. No clothing carelessly discarded, no jewelry on the bedside table. He snatched up the pillow beside his and buried his face in it. Drawing a deep breath through his nose, he searched for her scent. And when he found it, he smiled.

"I wasn't dreaming," he said. His mind immediately flashed back to the passion they'd shared in her bed. When he'd first kissed her, he was looking for some trace of their honeymoon night, certain she could jog his memory. But the moment he slipped inside her, he knew he'd never experienced such pleasure before.

Isabelle had lied to him, and he should be furious with her. But right now, he didn't really give a damn. Her motives were all that mattered and he knew Isabelle had never wanted a divorce. Had she loved him all along? Even when he was with Maggie? Or had it happened that night in the elevator when they'd shared a bottle of champagne?

There were plenty of hours and days and months left to answer all the questions he had. But he was anxious to get one thing cleared up—their divorce. As far as he was concerned, there would be no divorce. Their marriage would stand exactly as it was.

Colin crawled out of bed, grabbed his pants and

quickly tugged them on. Isabelle had probably gone to get breakfast. Or maybe she'd gone back to his room to shower. He crossed to the door, then pulled it open and walked into the hallway. His door was ajar and he wandered in without knocking.

"You're up early."

His voice startled her and she spun around, her hand pressed to her heart. She closed her eyes and drew in a deep breath. "I didn't want to wake you. I took a shower in here. I—I thought you could use the sleep."

He watched as she put the sweater he'd bought her into a new duffel bag. "What are you doing?"

"What does it look like?" she said in a cheery voice. "I'm packing. Check-out time is at ten."

He crossed the room and wrapped his arms around her waist, pulling her against his body. "When I woke up, you weren't there," he said, nuzzling her neck. "I thought I dreamed last night."

She slipped out of his embrace, retreating to the other side of the bed. "No, it wasn't a dream. It was very real."

He stared at her for a long moment, trying to read her mood, but she deftly avoided his gaze, going back to her packing. "Isabelle, about last night. I want you to know that—"

"I suppose you'll be anxious to get back to Chicago," she interrupted. "And I'm sure your parents will be happy to see you."

"Maybe," he said. "But I was thinking we wouldn't have to fly back today. We could stay a little longer if you want to. We have plenty of money left from the ring and we can change our plane tickets easily enough."

Isabelle shook her head. "I'm not going to stay." She paused. "And I'm not going back to Chicago. I've decided to take a little side trip to San Francisco. I know one of the costume designers at the San Francisco Opera and she always said if I'm ever in the area I should stop by. I don't have to be back to work until the end of January. So, I have some…time. For a vacation. I need some time to clear my head."

Colin frowned, stunned by her news. "So you're just going to leave? You're not coming home with me? What about last night?"

"What about it?" She carefully folded the T-shirt she'd worn that night at the Happy Jackrabbit and placed it in the bag.

"We made love, Isabelle."

She shrugged. "We had sex. We satisfied our curiosity. Now we'll never have to wonder what it might have been like. You remember and so do I."

"We know what it *could* be like, Isabelle. What it *is* like between us. Do you just want to walk away from that?"

"I—I have to." She glanced over at him, then looked away. "This would never work out between us. You know it and I know it. We're two completely different people with lives of our own."

"But that can be good," he said. "That *is* good."

"You need someone who can fit into your world. A woman your parents would approve of."

"Isabelle, I'm beginning to realize *I* don't even fit into my world. Hell, we can stay here in Mexico for the rest of our lives."

"And there are so many other things," she continued. "We're always fighting. We…irritate each other. And then there's the mark."

"The mark?"

"The mark of the millennium. You showed it to me last night." She paused. "Do you know Maggie has the same mark on her hand?"

He raked his fingers through his hair and shook his head, confused by her behavior. "What does that have to do with anything?"

"Maggie is your destiny. I got in the way of that. I was so sure you'd make a horrible husband, but I was wrong. You'll make Maggie a wonderful husband."

"But I don't love Maggie."

"But you could," Isabelle said. "And you will. You both have the mark."

He reached out and grabbed her arm, forcing her to look at him. "Damn it, Isabelle, listen to me."

"And you don't have to worry. I'll never tell Maggie what happened, I swear. It will be our secret. We'll get a nice quiet divorce and you can go back to the life you wanted. The life that was meant for you."

"That's not the life I want, Isabelle." He drew a deep breath. "The life I want is with you."

She looked up at him, her eyes wide, her lips parted. Then she slowly shook her head. "No. That can't be. I'm sorry, I can't be your wife, Colin. I—I don't want to be."

He took her face in his hands and stared into her eyes. "You already are my wife." Colin bent forward and touched his lips to hers in a kiss so sweet he wanted it to last forever. "We don't have to get a divorce. We'll go back to Chicago and announce to the world that we're married. It's as simple as that."

Isabelle looked up at him and, for an instant, he thought she might agree. But then she slowly pulled away, taking one step back and then another. "We'd both end up back in the same place in a few months. Maybe even a few weeks. So why not just end it now?"

Colin cursed beneath his breath, his frustration reaching the breaking point. If she was going to push, he'd push back. Harder. "All right, we'll end it. Right now. All you have to do is tell me you don't love me. Look into my eyes and say it, Isabelle. You owe me that much."

"The only thing I owe you is my signature on the divorce papers," she snapped. "Go back to Chicago and talk to your lawyer. I'll sign whatever I have to sign when I get back." She zipped up the duffel bag and hoisted it over her shoulder. "I have a shuttle to catch."

Colin followed her to the door and grabbed her arm to stop her. "Isabelle, don't do this. I can't believe you'd throw this all away because of some stupid little mark on my palm."

She laughed bitterly. "See, this is exactly what I'm talking about! Maybe I believe in what the fortuneteller had to say. But that doesn't matter to you. You can't bully me into thinking like you and acting like you."

"That's not what I'm trying to do. I don't give a damn if you believe in the man in the moon. But I'm hoping you could believe in us, too."

"There is no us," she said, tugging out of his grasp. "That's why divorce is the only answer."

She hurried down the colonnade, her footsteps sharp and quick on the Spanish tile. And then she disappeared down the steps to the courtyard. Colin stared after her, dumbfounded.

How the hell had things gone so bad in such a short time? After last night, he'd thought everything was settled between them. They'd made love. They belonged together. They'd forget about the divorce. He'd been sure of it, so sure he'd been willing to stake his future on it.

He walked slowly over to the railing and stared down into the courtyard below. This was not over—not by a long shot. If Isabelle Channing wanted a divorce, she'd have to fight him for it. He'd drag her into court and throw every obstacle in her way until she finally admitted to herself that she loved him.

It could get messy and be very public, but Colin didn't give a damn. He stood to lose a lot—his inheritance, his parents, maybe even some friends and business associates. He'd have to find another way to make a living and he'd probably have to give up his apartment.

But nothing he faced could possibly be worse than losing Isabelle Channing.

9

THE SHAKESPEARE THEATRE Company's costume
shop was dark and silent when Isabelle arrived. She
let herself into the workroom with her key, then
slowly strolled through the racks of costumes for *The
Merchant of Venice*, a new production opening in
mid-February. She plucked at bodices and hems, ex-
amining the stitching for the intricate gowns she had
designed for Portia.

She'd given her seamstresses time off with the
promise they would be required to work some eve-
nings and weekends in order to complete all the fit-
tings for the leads and the minor characters. The costumes would be fitted during the two-week
rehearsal period preceding opening night.

Isabelle plopped down on the chair at her worktable and idly flipped through a book of fabric sam-
ples. She'd been away for a week, yet it seemed as if
her job was part of a whole different life. She'd returned to Chicago after just a few days in San Francisco, restless to be home and settled. Ready to forget
what had happened since the eve of the millennium.
Although she hadn't the nerve to call Maggie yet.

But she couldn't forget. Time after time, her
thoughts slipped back to the wedding under the laser lights of Las Vegas…and the Happy Jackrabbit in
Skull Creek…and the quaint hotel in Tijuana. And

the settings always came complete with thoughts of Colin. Her mind would get stuck on images of him—sleeping in their big round bed in the High Rollers Suite, hauling her off the stage at the wet T-shirt contest, lying naked next to her in her room at the Hotel Florencia.

She'd been so certain she could forget him, just put him in the past and get on with her life...until she realized her love for him was not going to go away. Isabelle braced her chin in her hand and doodled on a drawing pad with a colored pencil, writing his name and her name over and over again in an elaborate hand.

Colin Spencer. Colin Spencer. Mrs. Colin Spencer. Isabelle Channing Spencer.

She groaned and tore the paper out of the drawing pad, crumpled it into a wad and threw it across the room. So she loved Colin Spencer. She hadn't realized how much, or how deeply, until she had walked out on him that day in Tijuana. The temptation to turn around and run back into his arms had been strong. Instead, she had marshaled every ounce of determination and left him, and their marriage, behind.

Yet, once she'd put some distance between them, everything began to change. The hard edges began to soften, the doubts began to recede, and she started to see Colin as something other than a threat to her happiness. He cared about her, he watched over her and made sure she was safe. In truth, she'd never been happier than in the few days she'd spent with Colin.

Every minute of every hour had been filled with excitement and exhilaration. She'd felt as if she was living her life in bright, bold colors, whirling through her days and nights with only her heart to guide her, pausing just long enough to take a breath before throwing herself back into their time together. Her day-to-day existence had paled in comparison.

She wanted to feel that way again, to hear her breath catch in her throat when he walked into the room, to feel her heart skip a beat when he touched her, and to have every worry slip from her mind when he kissed her. Isabelle groaned softly and buried her head in her hands. A knock on the door of the costume shop brought her bolting upright and she pasted a smile on her face.

"Isabelle?"

She recognized the softly accented voice of Delores Ruiz, the receptionist for the company's offices. "I'm back here," Isabelle called.

When she appeared from behind the racks of costumes, Delores smiled. "You have a visitor." She moved aside and Isabelle's breath froze in her throat as Colin stepped forward. "I'll just leave you two alone. I've got to get back to the phones."

Isabelle stood up, pressing her hand to her chest. Her heart beat a ragged rhythm. This was exactly how she wanted to feel, all silly and light-headed, as if she might just float away any minute. He looked incredibly attractive. Dressed in a suit and tie, he held a cashmere overcoat over his arm. His hair was combed, slicked back to reveal the startlingly handsome planes and angles of his face.

Though he looked cool and unapproachable, Isabelle couldn't help but recall the man who had shared her bed—the warm, passionate, sexy man who had made her blood run hot and her body ache with desire. Perhaps, if she reached out and undid his tie, slowly unbuttoned his crisp, white shirt, he might become that man again.

She swallowed hard, pushing aside her runaway thoughts. "What are you doing here?"

His eyebrow arched. "Why didn't you call and tell me you were back? I left messages on your machine."

"How did you find me?"

He carefully laid his coat over one of the costume racks. "We give a lot of money to the Shakespeare Theatre Company," he explained. "I called the director and promised him a sizable donation if he'd let me know when you returned. Ms. Ruiz was instructed to call me as soon as you came into work."

"Delores called you?" Isabelle bristled. How typical! Using his money to win friends and influence people—and to spy on her. She sat back down in her chair. "Well, you can leave. I have a lot of work to do and I don't have anything to say to you."

He took a step forward. "I have something to say to you, Isabelle."

She glanced up and met his gaze and, once again, her breath caught in her throat. Isabelle scolded herself inwardly. She'd have to stop looking at him or risk oxygen deprivation. "I don't have to listen," she said. "We're not married anymore, remember?"

A smile curled the corners of his mouth. "Actually, we are still married," he said. "That's why I'm here." He tossed a business card onto her drawing table. "It's the name of an attorney."

"What do I need an attorney for?"

"He'll represent you in the divorce proceedings. I'll cover his fee, so you don't have to worry about money." Colin cleared his throat, a grim expression fixed on his face. "I was going to fight this divorce, but then I decided not to. After all, if you don't think our marriage is worth saving, then I guess I don't either. But I do think you should try to get a fair settlement. We were married. Even if it was only for a few days, you deserve something for all your trouble."

"I—I don't want anything from you," she said. "I just want you out of my life."

"I'm a wealthy man, Isabelle, and I can certainly spare the expense. A settlement could give you financial security. And I think you could use that." He slowly withdrew an envelope from the breast pocket of his jacket and placed it on her drawing table. "But then, you could always go to your parents for help," he said.

"My parents?"

He pointed to the envelope. "After we ran off together, my parents hired a private investigator to look into your background. I guess they thought you might be some kind of gold digger intent on swindling me out of my fortune."

Isabelle swallowed hard. "And what did they find?"

He shrugged. "I don't know. I didn't read the report. I really don't care what it says. But my mother did convey one little bit of information. It seems your family has money. A lot of it."

She tipped her chin up. "You had no right to—"

He slammed his hands down on the worktable and leaned over, his expression dark and threatening. "Damn it, Isabelle. For once, be honest. Stop trying to hide behind all that bravado and bohemian bullshit and tell me the truth."

"All right," she said, her voice trembling. "You

want the truth. I'm rich. I'm not as rich as you are, but my family has loads and loads of money. And I'm the only child, so I stand to inherit a big share of the loot. Ever heard of the Detroit Channings? My father owns a couple of steel mills, some real estate and a garage full of very expensive cars. But since I haven't talked to my parents in over five years, I'm not real confident I'll be included in the will."

Colin stared at her for a long moment, then shook his head as if he wasn't sure he'd heard her right. "And all those times you made me feel guilty for being who I was. All those insults, and you knew exactly how I felt. You knew what I was going through."

"Money doesn't buy happiness," she said. "I escaped. You're still caught up in it. You see, for some people, like my parents, all that money built a nice little wall around their life, a wall to keep out people who were…undesirable. But for me, that wall was a prison. I was expected to behave a certain way, to speak a certain way. From the time I first started noticing boys, my mother was working out strategies to catch me a suitable—and very rich—husband."

"And I'm that suitable husband?"

"To my mother, you're the perfect husband," Isabelle said. "Too bad *she* didn't run off to Las Vegas with you."

"I'm confused," Colin said.

"About what? I've made everything very clear."

"This whole thing, denying your feelings, pushing me away. This doesn't have anything to do with you and me. It has everything to do with your mother. And maybe your father, too."

"That's ridiculous."

"No, I don't think it is. You're so damn determined to reject everything your parents offered you, that you're willing to throw away something that has nothing to do with them."

"And what about you?" she asked. "When you got onto that elevator with me, you were terrified you were about to turn into your father. We're not so different, you and I."

"You don't want to become your mother, is that it?" he said. Colin laughed harshly. "That's just some stupid excuse you've cooked up in your mind to rationalize why you can't be with me. You're great with excuses, aren't you, Isabelle? The money, your mother, this stupid mark on my hand. You're just so wrapped up in your excuses you can't see how much better it could be if we were together." He drew a long breath, then met her gaze, his eyes intense. "We could have made it work, Isabelle. But you obviously don't want to make the effort. As far as I'm concerned, we're through." He grabbed his coat from where he'd dropped it and tossed it back over his arm. "I'll have my attorney draw up the papers for an uncontested divorce. Once they're signed, you'll be free to get back to your wonderful life and I'll be free to get on with mine."

He turned on his heel and then disappeared into the costume racks. Isabelle drew a long, ragged breath, trying to control the trembling in her body. But when tears sprang to the corners of her eyes and ran down her cheeks, she couldn't push aside her emotions. A sob slipped from her throat and she covered her face with her hands.

Why did she try so hard to alienate him? She was supposed to love him! Yet whenever they were together, she did everything in her power to drive him away. He'd done nothing but love and protect her and she'd rejected him at every turn.

"I'm such an idiot," she said. "I married a man I hated and now I'm divorcing the man I love."

Fresh tears ran down her cheeks and she brushed at them with impatient fingers. Maybe Colin was right. It was time for honesty. And time to stop with the excuses. Telling him she loved him couldn't be more painful than not telling him. But it was what came after the "I love yous" that frightened her.

Could she be Mrs. Colin Spencer for the rest of her life?

COLIN STOOD at the wide wall of windows spanning two sides of the Spencer Center penthouse. He stared out at the skyline of Chicago, stark and colorless against the gray winter clouds. The weather matched his mood. In truth, since he'd returned from Mexico, the sunshine seemed to have disappeared from his life altogether.

He'd gone right back to work without missing a step, settling into meetings and negotiations as if he'd never been away. Of course, Eunice and Edward had been hovering over him, questioning him about his absence, demanding to know his plans regarding his aborted engagement.

Right now, Colin didn't want to make any plans. He still hadn't completely given up hope that Isabelle might come to her senses and realize they belonged together. He had all the papers in his possession, all ready to sign and put an end to their marriage. But he hadn't called her.

In truth, Colin was determined to give it one more

shot. There had to be a way to convince Isabelle to give him a chance to make her happy. He'd gone over their conversation of the previous afternoon, trying to understand her reasoning, searching for a chink in her armor.

She loved him—he had to believe that. And if she loved him, then there was a way to her heart. He just needed the time to figure out the correct route, the right reasoning and logic to make her see what he had seen all along—they could make a future together.

But before he tackled his problems with his wife, he had other problems to resolve with his fiancée. Footsteps sounded on the parquet floor and echoed through the cavernous interior of the reception area. He slowly turned to see Maggie Kelley crossing the room. He'd sent Hamilton, the Spencer family chauffeur to her shop just that morning, requesting she meet him and, in typical fashion, Maggie had complied.

How different she and Isabelle were. In the years they were together, he and Maggie never fought. He'd thought it meant they were in love, a perfect relationship without any flaws. But after living with Isabelle for four days, he knew the lack of emotion in his relationship with Maggie would have destroyed their marriage sooner or later.

As Maggie approached, he tried to read her expression, searching for anger or bitterness, prepared to placate her with all manner of excuses. But all he saw was a sweet and very genuine smile. Her eyes were bright and her color high and she looked more beautiful, more radiant than he remembered.

Still, all her beauty did nothing to stir the desires in

him. Not like Isabelle, who could send him a re-
proachful look and make his gut twist with need and
his mind turn to mush. Colin cleared his throat and
forced a smile. "Thanks for coming," he said when
she'd joined him at the window.

Maggie tucked an errant strand of pale blond hair
behind her ear. "I—I wasn't sure I should," she replied, glancing around. She rubbed her arms and
shivered. "This place looks a lot different than it did
a week ago."

Colin bent over and picked up a scrap of silver net-
ting from the floor, then rubbed it between his fingers. "Maggie, let me get right to the point. I know
what I did was hurtful and I won't blame you if you
never forgive me, but—"

She held up her hand to stop his apology. "But I do
forgive you," she said.

"You do?"

"You did what you had to do. There's no wrong in
that."

He turned and stared out the windows again, completely taken aback by her admission. "You might
not say that once you hear the whole story." Colin
started at the beginning, with the elevator and the
bottle of champagne. And when he ended with Isabelle walking out on him in Tijuana, he was certain
Maggie would hate him for the rest of her life. Hell,
he'd run out on his fiancée and married her best
friend. What woman wouldn't detest him? When he
finally had the courage to look at her, Maggie was
smiling.

"You and Isabelle are married?" she said, her disbelief mixed with amusement.

Colin nodded. "For now. But she's determined to divorce me so I can marry you."

Maggie laughed out loud. "Let's be honest, Colin. We never should have agreed to marry each other. We don't belong together. And if you hadn't run out that night, I probably would have. Believe me, I thought about it more than once. And Isabelle knew that. She knew we weren't meant to be together and I think she set out to prove it."

"I know she did," Colin said. "And that's probably why we ended up married. It seems what Isabelle wants, Isabelle gets, especially when it comes to me. She thought a wedding between us would be so unforgivable you'd never speak to me again."

"But I'm speaking to you now."

"Unfortunately, she's changed her opinion on our relationship." He held up his hand and pointed to the base of his thumb.

Maggie's eyes brightened and she gasped in surprise. "The mark of the millennium? But Madame Blavatka said it was very rare."

"That's probably all part of her act. Isabelle thinks it means you and I belong together. Destiny and all that. She has some very strange ideas and doesn't always operate from a rational point of view."

Maggie shook her head. "She also didn't listen to the fortune-teller. This mark is supposed to mean you belong with whomever you were with at midnight on the eve of the millennium. I take it that was Isabelle?"

Colin frowned. "It was. So according to the fortune-teller, *Isabelle* is my destiny?"

"If you believe in fortune-tellers," Maggie said. "I'm not sure I do."

Colin reached out and took her hands. "Who were you with at midnight, Maggie?"

She blushed, a pretty pink staining her pale cheeks. "I was with Luke. He was really sweet and he helped me through everything. And over the past week, we've become...very close."

"Do you love him?"

She nodded. "I do. I just realized it on the drive over here and now I might be too late."

"Why?"

"He left this morning for Albania and I don't know when he'll be back. Or if he'll be back. We didn't leave things on very good terms."

"But you love him."

Maggie nodded. "I guess I always have, ever since we were kids. But I'm not sure Luke is ready to settle down." She sighed. "I thought love would be so easy. That's why I thought I was in love with you. I know now it's all very difficult."

Colin gave her hands a squeeze. "And I always suspected you and Luke would be good together. He cares about you, Maggie. And he'd never do anything to hurt you. That counts for a lot. He'll come back, and when he does, give him a chance."

"And what about you?" Maggie asked. "Are you going to be all right?"

"I spent four days with Isabelle Channing. We've seen the absolute worst in each other. We've been to hell and back. And I still love her. I just have to convince her she loves me."

Maggie giggled. "That's not going to be easy. Isabelle can be very stubborn. Especially if she thinks you're trying to tell her what to do."

"I know she's worried about you, about how you

are. Do you think you can still be friends?" Colin asked.

"She saved my life," Maggie replied. "She knew I didn't want to marry you and she did everything she could to keep a wedding from happening." Maggie looked up into Colin's eyes. "I guess maybe I should return the favor."

"What do you mean?"

"I mean, maybe I should save *her* life."

"And how will you do that?"

Maggie smiled coyly. "While you were gone, I learned a few things. From your mother of all people."

"My mother?"

"Eunice was convinced you were going to come back and marry me. She wouldn't take no for an answer. So I think we should use some of her techniques to convince Isabelle you *are* going to marry me after all."

"You want to pretend we're going to get married?"

"Isabelle stopped our wedding plans once. If she really loves you, she'll stop them again." Maggie grinned. "I know Isabelle. And I think my little plan will work."

ISABELLE STOOD in the corner of the elevator and watched as the numbers on the panel above the door ascended from the ground floor to the penthouse level of the Spencer Center. It wasn't until she was passing the thirtieth floor that she realized this was the very car she and Colin had occupied on New Year's Eve.

She'd received a call from her soon-to-be ex-husband that morning with news that he had the divorce papers and they were ready to sign. After she hung up the phone, she'd cursed herself for not letting the machine pick up the call. She'd wanted to dodge his calls for a few more days while she tried to find a way to apologize to him, a way to repair the damage she had done.

But it was too late. Any love Colin had for her was probably long forgotten. Once again, she'd managed to ruin another relationship with a man. Only this time, it was with a man she loved. It would take a long time to forget, if she ever did. And Isabelle knew the regrets would haunt her for the rest of her life.

She could have been happy with him. And though there were risks in any marriage, with a little compromise, they might have worked their differences out. Colin might have learned to be more understanding. And Isabelle knew she could be less headstrong if she tried. "But it's too late," she murmured.

The doors opened in front of her and, for a second, she hesitated. Isabelle had dreaded this day for a long time—at least it seemed like a lifetime, though it had only been a little more than a week. She knew they'd have to put an end to their marriage, but no matter how hard she tried, she couldn't dispel that tiny sliver of hope that remained. If she saw even the slightest hint of love in his eyes, then it wasn't completely over. She'd gather her courage and admit her feelings. And if all went well, maybe she could salvage what they'd shared.

Drawing a deep breath, she stepped out of the elevator into the wide lobby of the penthouse reception hall. The place was completely empty, the silence echoing off the high ceilings and polished wooden floor. The doors to the hall were open and she peeked inside. Her breath stilled as she saw a solitary figure, silhouetted against the windows by the afternoon sun.

Even the sight of him from such a distance affected her so deeply. She felt as if they were still connected by some unspoken and unseen bond, a bond that had nothing to do with the crazy wedding they'd had or the unique honeymoon. This was a man who had come to know her in just a few short days. And even after he knew her, he'd still had the capacity to love her, no matter how hard she tried to push him away.

Isabelle took a step into the hall and then another. As she walked toward him, she looked around, surprised to see decorations scattered around the room. Everything seemed mismatched with different colors and schemes in different corners. Three or four tables had been laid out with varying floral centerpieces, fine china and crisply starched linens.

When she finally brought her gaze back to Colin, she found him watching her. The slightest hint of a smile touched his lips, but his expression remained cool and distant. She could detect nothing in his gaze. "I'm glad you came," he said.

Isabelle twisted her fingers together in front of her then glanced around, eager to keep her eyes from meeting his. "What's all this?"

"Oh, nothing. Just some things for a wedding reception." He gently took her arm and pulled her toward a table. "I've got the papers over here. This will only take a minute or two and then you can be on your way."

Reluctantly, Isabelle sat down in the chair he offered and looked at the documents spread out in front of her. This was it. This was the end of her marriage to Colin Spencer, here in these papers filled with confusing legalese and parties of the first and second part. Colin held out a pen and she took it with trembling fingers.

"Where do I sign?"

He braced his hand on the table beside her and reached over her shoulder, leaning so close she could feel the warmth radiating from his body. "Right here," he said, his breath teasing at her ear. She followed his finger to a spot at the bottom of the first page, then numbly watched as her hand scribbled her name, unable to stop herself.

Colin leaned closer as he turned to the next page. "And here," he said.

Once again, she signed her name. And again and again until Colin had run out of papers and she had run out of resolve. She wanted to reach up and touch him, to run her fingers along his strong jaw, to trace a line across his lips. Surely just one kiss wouldn't hurt, would it? If she turned her face up to his and closed her eyes, would he accept the invitation?

Isabelle reached out and arranged the papers in a neat stack. When she'd finished, he grabbed them up, folded them haphazardly and stuck them in the breast pocket of his suit jacket. She glanced up at his face, hoping to see some glint of emotion there, just the tiniest hint of regret. But his features were bland. "I—I guess that's it, then," she said.

He nodded. "I guess so. That wasn't too difficult, was it?"

"No," she lied. In truth, she'd never had to do anything as heartrending and soul-shattering as letting Colin Spencer go. But this was for the best. In her mind, she knew that. She only had to convince her heart. With a soft sigh, she stood up and rebuttoned her coat. "Well, I guess I should go. I mean, if that's all there is."

She wasn't going to say goodbye. Isabelle wasn't sure she'd even be able to get the words out without the tears as well. She started toward the doors, but his voice stopped her, the sound of her name echoing louder than her footsteps. For an instant, hope sprang to life in her heart. He wasn't going to let her go through with this. He was going to stop her...and she was going to let him. Slowly, she turned around, her heart slamming in her chest.

"As long as you're here," he said, "maybe you can give me some advice. What do you think of these centerpieces?" He stood in front of a line of four tables and rubbed his chin thoughtfully. "I don't know which one I like the best."

Isabelle frowned. Floral centerpieces at a time like this? What could be going through his mind? "I—I think they're all beautiful," she said, taking a step toward him. "White roses are always pretty. So are lilies. Why do you ask?"

He shrugged. "I just needed a woman's opinion. I want to make sure everything is perfect."

"Perfect? For what?"

"For the wedding," he said.

Isabelle stared at him, dumbfounded, unable to believe what she was hearing. "Wha—what wedding?"

"My wedding. I have to choose the invitations, too. I can't decide between the white or the buff." He grabbed a huge book from one of the tables and held it out to her. "What do you think?"

"You're getting married?" Isabelle asked, her heart twisting in her chest and a strange buzzing invading her head. "You and—and Maggie? You worked things out?"

"Maggie is very forgiving," he said. "I told her all about what happened and she was fine with it. She laughed. In fact, she wants you to call her."

"Me? Call Maggie?"

"I don't think she has any hard feelings at all. In fact, she told me she was completely in love. I think you'll come out of this the very best of friends. Now, what do you think of this invitation? This is more a cream color, which is much less…how would you say, stuffy? Pompous? Or what is the word you liked to use? Constipated?"

"I really think the bride should choose," she said, backing away from him in disbelief.

"Hmm. Well, maybe you're right. But which one would you choose?"

His tone was insistent, so insistent Isabelle wanted to scream. How could he do this to her? How could he be so blasé about marrying Maggie when he'd just divorced her? He was cruel and heartless and he didn't deserve an ounce of her affection!

Angry, Isabelle grabbed the book of invitations from him and briskly flipped through the pages until she came upon a wedding invitation she could almost like. "This one," she said, jabbing her finger at it. "But I wouldn't use flowery script. Just something plain."

"Good choice," Colin said. "I like this one."

"Now, if we're through, I'd like to—"

"If you don't mind, you could help me with a few other things. There are some dresses I'd like—"

Isabelle gasped. "Dresses? You want me to look at wedding dresses? Are you crazy? I—"

"Actually, Maggie thought you might have some opinions on bridesmaid dresses."

"No," Isabelle said stubbornly. "I—I can't do this. I can't help you plan your wedding."

"But you have such a good fashion sense. And this will only take a few minutes. I'd really value your opinion."

He took her hand in his and led her to a rack positioned near the door. It was filled with colorful gowns and Isabelle's heart fell as she saw the wedding dresses hanging on one end. One of those dresses was Maggie's. She'd wear it as she walked down the aisle and became Mrs. Colin Spencer.

Isabelle's fists clenched at her side. But *she* was Mrs. Colin Spencer! Isabelle Channing Spencer. She was the one who was supposed to have a happily-ever-after with Colin! Not Maggie!

"I see you noticed the wedding gowns," he said. He pulled one off the rack and held it up. "What do you think?"

Isabelle sniffed disdainfully as she examined the dress. "Little Bo-Peep," she said.

He wrinkled his nose. "You're right. How about this one?"

She shook her head. "Scarlett O'Hara."

"Absolutely." He ran his hand along the rack. "In fact, I don't like any of these."

"Can I go now?" Isabelle asked. "Or are we going to listen to wedding music next?"

Colin smiled. "Just one more thing." He grabbed a

looseleaf folder from a nearby table and held it out to her. "Cakes," he said. "I never knew there were so many choices. At least one choice was simple." He held out a small box. "Open it."

Warily, Isabelle took the box and lifted the lid. Amidst a cloud of tissue paper, she found a delicate porcelain bride and groom. She took the pretty china figurine in her hand. She wanted to smash it on the floor and stomp all over the shards. But she couldn't. This is what Colin wanted and she had to be brave enough to accept it.

"What do you think?" he asked. "It's for the top of the cake."

"It's nice," she murmured. "Except the bride has the wrong color hair."

"No," Colin said. "This is right. This is exactly what I ordered."

"But Maggie has blond hair," Isabelle countered.

"Maggie?"

"Yes, Maggie. Your bride. The woman you're planning this wedding for."

Colin chuckled and shook his head. "Where would you get an idea like that? I'm not marrying Maggie."

"But you said—"

"I never said I was marrying Maggie."

"Then who?"

He grinned. "Who do you think?"

She stared down at the porcelain bride and groom, then looked up at Colin. Her lower lip trembled and she felt tears push at the corners of her eyes. She opened her mouth to speak, but nothing came out, her throat clotted with emotion. Could this be true? Was he giving her one more chance?

"Who do you think, Isabelle? Who is the only woman I'll ever consider marrying? Who is the woman I love and adore, the woman I want to grow old with? And who is the woman who will give me children and make my life complete?"

"Me?" The word came out like a squeak, her voice cracking with the effort.

He hooked his thumb under her chin. "You. All of this is for you. And if you don't like it, we'll start over again. We'll plan and plan, until we get it exactly right. If you want to get married in the middle of Michigan Avenue during a blizzard, I'll make it happen. I want our wedding to be perfect."

"But we're already married," she said.

"Not anymore. You signed the papers," he said, patting the breast pocket of his suit. "Once they're signed, we're divorced. And now that we're divorced, I thought we could start all over again. Get it right from the very beginning. After all, there are going to have to be some changes made. I'm going to have to be—"

"More understanding," she said. "And more spontaneous. And more broad-minded and tolerant."

"Is that all?"

Isabelle felt a blush warm her cheeks. "But I promise to try to be well behaved and cooperative and agreeable."

"Agreeable? Does that mean you'll marry me all over again?"

Isabelle slipped her hand into his jacket and pulled out the divorce papers. Slowly, she tore them to ribbons and tossed them over her shoulder. "I don't need to marry you again, Colin Spencer. I'm already married to you."

Colin grinned and swept her into his arms, spinning her around and around until she was dizzy with delight. Then he put her down and kissed her thoroughly. When he finally drew back, he gazed into her eyes. "Maggie said this would work."

Isabelle blinked in surprise. "Maggie?"

"She said you saved her life when you lured me to Las Vegas. So she helped me plan this all. She said she wanted to return the favor."

Isabelle tipped her head back and laughed, the sound bouncing off the ceiling and walls until the entire room was filled with her happiness. "I do love you, Colin Spencer. I don't know why, but I do."

"And I love you, Isabelle Channing Spencer." He kissed her once more, long and hard, erasing any shred of doubt she might have. Then he reached in his pocket and withdrew a small box. "I think we should make it official," he said, flipping open the top.

He pulled a diamond ring from the box and held it out in front of her. As soon as Isabelle saw it, she recognized it. It was *her* ring, the one he'd given her in the parking lot of the Fashion Show Mall in Las Vegas. He slipped it on her trembling finger and she gazed up at him.

"This is back where it belongs," he said. "On your finger."

She wrapped her arms around his neck and hugged him hard. Closing her eyes, she reveled in his warm embrace, unwilling to ever let him go again. The new millennium had brought so many unexpected changes to her life. In just a week, she'd become a different woman—a woman who could love without inhibition or doubt. A woman who had years of happiness to look forward to.

She stared at her hand, her chin resting on his shoulder, the diamond glinting in the light from the windows. "And I'm back where I belong," she murmured. "Where I've always belonged."

_____ Epilogue _____

TTHE CORK POPPED and champagne bubbled over the neck of the bottle. Isabelle watched as Colin carefully filled the four crystal flutes on the table in front of him. He held up his glass, the bubbles sparkling in the soft candlelight, then looked over and smiled at her. A delicious shiver skittered down her spine as she caught the sexy glint in his eye, the suggestive arch of his eyebrow.

Their "official" wedding had only been three months ago, yet the honeymoon didn't show signs of ending anytime soon. Later that night, they'd share a private celebration in Colin's apartment downstairs, but now they sat at a small table in front of the wide window of the Spencer Center penthouse, waiting for midnight.

Below, the city glittered, pulsing with the excitement of another celebration. Unlike the previous New Year's Eve, this year the party in the penthouse consisted of only four guests—Isabelle and Colin and their old friends, Maggie and Luke Fitzpatrick. A sumptuous dinner had been laid out before them by the caterer and soft music echoed through the hall from a violinist Colin had hired.

After all that had passed between the four of them, it was a wonder they were still speaking. But Isabelle and Maggie had quickly repaired their friendship, and though Maggie and Luke lived in northern Wisconsin, the two women spoke often on the phone. In June, Isabelle had served as Maggie's maid of honor and Maggie had returned the favor for Isabelle's October wedding.

As for Colin and Luke, they still were a bit wary around each other. But the happiness they'd found with the women they loved had caused past resentments to fade slowly and their old friendship soon strengthened.

Colin stood up, then tipped his glass to his guests. "After last year, I guess spending New Year's Eve together has become a bit of a tradition with us," he began.

"We didn't exactly spend last New Year's Eve together," Luke said.

"Well, we tried. But fate stepped in. The way I see it, this place is lucky for all of us. If I hadn't gotten stuck in the elevator with Isabelle, Luke would have never saved Maggie from a bad marriage."

"Don't be so sure," Luke teased. "I think I probably would have stolen her away from you before you actually tied the knot."

"And if I hadn't invited Isabelle to the party," Maggie said, "you never would have gotten stuck in the elevator."

"So," Colin said. "I guess we owe a good portion of our happiness to each other. The millennium was lucky for all of us." He tipped his glass to Luke and Maggie and the crystal rang like a chime. "To those we love and to many New Year's Eves to come."

Luke slipped his arm around Maggie's shoulder and nuzzled her cheek. And Colin sat down and covered Isabelle's hand with his, staring deeply into her eyes. They all took a sip of champagne and Isabelle knew everyone at the table was thinking about the strange turns that their lives had taken exactly a year ago at the stroke of midnight.

And though neither Luke nor Colin were expecting any more surprises, Maggie and Isabelle had shared their own good news earlier that evening, news they'd tell their husbands later, when they were alone. By next New Year's Eve there would be six at the table—the two newest additions drinking formula instead of champagne.

Isabelle wondered how Colin's parents would react to the news of a grandchild. Although they'd initially been shocked by their son's marriage to Isabelle, their feelings had been tempered by the knowledge that she came from a "good" family. And though she and Colin had made it clear they would live their life as they pleased, without regard for the opinion of the older Spencers, Isabelle knew her child would be welcomed into the family with great happiness.

Isabelle smiled to herself, then brushed a soft kiss on her husband's lips. Turning to Maggie, she gave her a wink, carefully setting her champagne flute on the table. Maggie smiled and did the same.

As Colin counted down the seconds to the new year, Isabelle looked around the table, her heart filling with joy. Everything had changed the moment she'd stepped into that elevator with Colin. At the time, she'd only hoped she was doing the right thing. But as she watched the love between Maggie and Luke and felt the same overwhelming passion for her husband, Isabelle knew.

The millennium had only brought good things to all of them. And when they were old, with their children grown, they would look back on that one night in time, that special moment, and remember the very instant that love worked its magic and changed their destiny forever.

Temptation®

COMING NEXT MONTH

#765 BILLY AND THE KID Kristine Rolofson
Bachelors & Babies

Everyone in Cowman's Corner, Montana, believed the baby left on Will "Billy" Wilson's doorstep was his. And Will wasn't saying otherwise. So when Daisy McGregor agreed to help him look after "the kid," she knew she was risking her heart. Because she was looking for a family kind of man—and Will had *no* plans to be a daddy or a husband.

#766 MILLION DOLLAR VALENTINE Rita Clay Estrada

Mall exec Blake Wright really needed to loosen up. Who better to help out than Crystal Tynan, masseuse and free spirit? Except she seemed to rub him the wrong way…especially when she started getting overly creative with the window dressing of her aunt's flower shop. Still, there *was* a sizzling attraction…and it *was* Valentine's Day.

#767 VALENTINE FANTASY Jamie Denton

Fantasy For Hire…*Your pleasure is our business!* Newspaper reporter Cait Sullivan was determined to expose this unusual company as a sham, even if it meant going undercover. But once she met sexy-as-sin owner Jordan McBride, all she could think about was getting him "under the covers"….

#768 BARING IT ALL Sandra Chastain
Sweet Talkin' Guys

Reporter Sunny Clary was on a mission—to disclose the true identity of legendary male stripper Lord Sin. Only, every path led her to sexy playboy Ryan Malone. But it was her reaction to the two men that had her confused. Lord Sin made her yearn…. Ryan Malone made her burn…. How could she be drawn to such completely different men? *Or were they so different?*

CNM0100

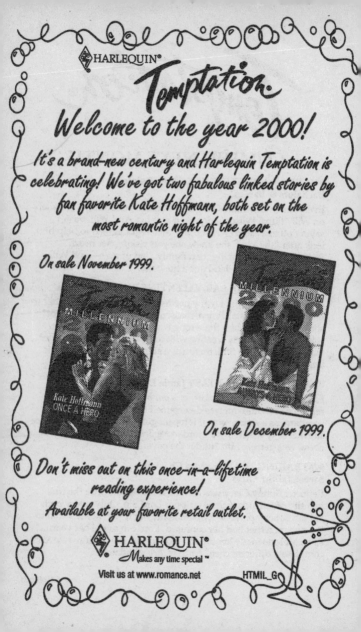